BEGGARMAN BOB

The Story of One Man's Enduring Legacy

By
DAVE STREGE

 Walking 4 Kids Books

http://www.walking4kids.com

BEGGARMAN BOB is a work of fiction. Events, characters, and incidents in this book are the product of the author's imagination, or are used fictitiously. Any resemblance to real persons, living or dead, is purely coincidental.

Cover Photo by Marilou Smith.

ISBN: 0-984-0475-0-6
ISBN 13: 978-0-9840475-0-5

1. Fiction: Christian 2.Ficiton: Inspirational

**Follow Dave Strege's adventure at
http://www.walking4kids.com**

Printed in the United States by Morris Publishing®
3212 East Highway 30
Kearney, NE 68847
1-800-650-7888

This book is dedicated to my three wonderful children, Anna, Chris, and Joseph.

ACKNOWLEDGEMENTS

The author wishes to acknowledge the contributions of Marilou Smith and Ed and Gail Lewis. These three gifted people surely had an abundance of other things to do besides helping me put this book together. Yet each of them gave freely of their time and talent. Without them, this book wouldn't exist and I thank God for their kind assistance.

PREFACE

All worthwhile things begin with a vision. The vision of walking4kids.com represents the convergence of multiple facets of my life, past, present and future.

Looking back, I've realized that every since my youth I have felt compassion for those who are poor through no fault of their own. In the past thirty years I have spent time visiting orphanages in Haiti, Mexico, and Africa. I have also visited several homes for trouble children here in the United States. I have seen way to many kids that do not have security or love and, worst of all, they lack the hope for a better future.

Being hungry and not having a place to shelter you at night is a very sad thing. Having no hope makes it almost unbearable. In each of the places I visited, I came away impressed by the amazing sacrifice and dedication of those people who work to make life better for youngsters who'd been dealt a pretty raw deals in life. These orphanages and homes offer children a stable environment, love and hope.

Moving into the present, despite the suffering of the world's children, life was pretty good for me in January, 2011. I was living comfortably on the beautiful southern Oregon Coast where I enjoyed golfing and kayaking, the people and the weather. I planned to retire there the following August and spend my days leisurely doing whatever I wanted. Everything seemed to be going for me. I should have been happy, yet I wasn't. My life lacked focus. Fortunately, God gave me that focus at a church service on January 16, 2011 and everything suddenly snapped into place.

And now to the future. Like a lot of people, I had always wanted to write a novel. As my ideas coalesced, I developed a plan. First, I would write that book...which I have now done. When it was finished, I'd promote it by walking and hitchhiking across the United States. I still planned to retire in August. But now, instead of sauntering across the golf course, I'll be making my way across the United States, sleeping under the stars in a tent and cooking over a campfire as I travel coast-to-coast promoting my book. My goal is to cover 12,000 miles in two years while writing additional books based on my experiences.

As I sojourn the highways and byways of America, I plan to talk to people about my book. I will speak at churches, schools, libraries, civic groups and any place else where someone will listen to me. One hundred percent of the proceeds from the books I sell while on the road will go to helping kids.

So here I am, 62-years-old with two previous heart attacks and arthritic knees as I begin to wind up my affairs and pack my backpack. Sound crazy? Many have told me it is. I'll tell you what I tell them. I'm going to see America the way I've always wanted to see her, and in the process help a lot kids who go to bed hungry every night with no hope of things getting any better.

Wish me well. Follow my adventures on the internet at http://www.walking4kids.com. When you think of it, say a prayer for me, and one other thing. Buy a book...it's for a good cause.

Dave Strege
Walking4kids.com

"I walk slowly, but I never walk backward."
— Abraham Lincoln

"Aim at heaven and you will get earth thrown in. Aim at earth and you get neither."
— C. S. Lewis

"Each of them is Jesus in disguise."
— Mother Teresa

CHAPTER 1

The sun was setting and there was a wonderful golden hue on the Western sky of Northern Arizona. He had been walking since sun up and was tired and looked forward to finding a place to bed down for the night. A secluded spot off the road, far enough away so that he could build a small campfire.

One of the many things that brought him enjoyment when on the road was a small fire on a cool night. Some nights he would get the bonus of a panoramic view, with the moon and stars, seeing a jet fly over, a satellite or shooting star. As long as he wasn't real hungry or thirsty, he had grown to love these times of tranquilly and peace.

It hadn't always been that way. At first when he decided to make the road his home, he was extremely lonely and on most nights he slept sporadically. Sleeping was difficult because he seldom had a comfortable bed to sleep on. When you don't have a mat of any kind, your mattress is what you can make of it from your environment. Most of the time the best he could do was to gather some leaves or grass together for a little padding. More often than not, he lay on the bare ground by his fire.

He carried a 4' x 8' sheet of plastic. When it wasn't raining, it was under him and over him when it was. He also carried a small blanket that he would fold in half so that he laid on one half and covered with the other.

Another thing that was a real detriment to a successful night's sleep was the sounds of the night. At first these sounds made sleep difficult. He was amazed how things would come to life after the sun quit giving off its wonderful light. He was on the road several weeks before he was able to be comfortable with these noisy, nocturnal creatures. By and large this group was made up of insects, lots and lots of insects. Some made way too much noise and some were totally silent. They walked, crawled and flew. Some would bite a little, but most didn't.

He did a majority of his traveling in the spring and fall, so he missed most of the mosquitoes that could be so tormenting. He learned to live with a few insect bites and after awhile he didn't let them rob him of sleep just because they might be checking him out or sharing his humble little bed. It took longer to adjust to things bigger than insects. At first he was sure that there was a whole host of man-eating animals just waiting for him to doze off so that they could attack him. He was pretty sure raccoons, skunks, and opossum would not cause too much damage before he woke up and beat them off, but what about the big ones? Animals like mountain lions, wolves, coyotes, bears, wild dogs, bob cats, and others he didn't even know about. Any sound at all in the dark was magnified in his ears and his mind to the point that he was sure that whatever it was that was making that noise was huge and had very large teeth and claws and was planning to do him some very serious harm for daring to invade its territory.

After many sleepless nights worrying about these horrifying sounds, he started checking for tracks of these killers when he got up in the morning. To his amazement he was unable to find anything but small tracks which he learned were mice, squirrels, raccoons, skunks, and opossums. He was sure that something much bigger was making all that noise at night.

In time he realized his fear was in his mind and not worth being constantly tired from staying awake most of the night. Out of habit, even after he quit worrying so much about man-eaters, he would check for tracks before he went to sleep and when he woke up in the morning. Over the years he noticed that he had some very interesting visitors while he slept. He had seen tracks of black bear, mountain lion, bob cat, coyote, deer, elk, cattle, sheep, and some he was not sure of. After awhile he realized that the only time he had seen most of these tracks close to his camp was when there was a breeze or wind, and the tracks were on the up wind side of him. It became clear that if these animals could smell him, they would give him a wide berth. They did not want anything to do with him and when he realized this, he started sleeping a lot better.

Over the years there were a few times when he would wake and go through his daily ritual of checking tracks for visitors and he would come across something that would send shivers up his spine. Human tracks...

There is an unwritten rule that when you come upon another man's camp you either go way around it or you announce yourself from a distance and ask for permission to come into camp. Sharing a camp on the road is not uncommon but most of the people out there would just as soon not fall asleep with someone in camp they didn't know or trust.

Bob was always very careful in picking his camp sites, and on some occasions he would stay for more than one night just because the site appealed to him. Those were sites that had water, trees, and a view if possible, but the most important thing was privacy. The only time he would join someone was because he recognized them from the past and not only trusted them, but liked them. This did not happen very often, but when it did, it was a nice break from being totally alone for days and weeks at a time.

Thousands of people, all over America, go north for the summer and south for the winter months and travel in the spring and fall. Most of us do not notice these nomadic people too much unless they cause a problem. A majority of those leading this transient lifestyle do what they can to keep a low profile because they do not want to have to deal with a police officer who may have a real dislike for road people. They can make your life pretty miserable if they want to. The usual is to take transients into the police station to hold them for awhile to make sure they have no warrants out for their arrest. If their record is clean, they are released and they make their way back to the road. Bob didn't have much of a problem with the police as he kept cleaner than most and always had identification with him. He was always just passing through. Staying calm and talking without acting guilty or crazy helped. He even got to know a state trooper in Southern Montana, who, after the first couple of times checking his identification, would stop and just talk to him and see how he was doing.

One man who Bob got to know was Sergeant Sam. Sam was a Vietnam veteran who lived off the road about 100 yards in a thicket of brush by a little creek that had water in it for six or seven months out of the year. Sam was a full timer as he lived there year round. When Bob would see him on the road he would end up going to his camp for the night because he liked him and they actually had a lot in common. On one of these occasions they were sitting around Sam's camp fire drinking coffee and cooking their dinner when a state trooper announced he was coming into camp. Bob figured he was coming to bust up Sam's camp and make both of them move down the road, but as soon as he came into camp, he greeted Sam, shook his hand and asked how he was doing.

"Jerry this is my friend Bob." Sam gestured toward Bob.

Jerry extended his hand saying, "Glad to meet you Bob."

"Would you like a cup?" Sam asked raising his coffee pot.

"No thanks, I just came by to see how you are doing. I need to get back on the road."

The officer looked at both of them, nodded his head and said, "It was good seeing both of you men," and walked out of camp.

Sam saw the puzzled look on Bob's face and said, "Jerry stopped me on the road a few years back. When he found out I was harmless, and that I was a Nam vet, he told me to get in his patrol car and gave me a ride to my camp. He dropped me off and asked if I minded if he checked on me every once in awhile. I told him he was welcome in my camp anytime. I learned later that Jerry's dad was killed in Nam when Jerry was only three years old, so he never really knew him. He told me that his memories of his dad stayed strong, mainly because of his mom's love for him. He told me she always made sure he knew what a good guy his dad was."

As Sam poured himself another cup of coffee he added, "In the summer, when it's hot, Jerry always brings a gallon of water with him when he visits me. I am lucky to have him as a friend and his dad would be proud of him."

Bob nodded his head and the two men turned toward the campfire and their thoughts were lost in the flames.

Another vet who Bob would run into once in awhile was an unusual man who rode a three-wheeled bicycle from his camp to town and back. He had a basket on the back of his three-wheeler to carry his belongings in and he always had an American flag on a short pole attached to that basket. He also always had head phones on listening to rock and roll music from the sixties. Along with the flag and head phones he always was smiling and waved at everyone. Bob never stayed in his camp, but always greeted him and he would greet Bob like he knew him. Bob never really knew if he really recognized him or was just greeting him like he did everyone else. He went by the name of R&R Flagman.

Every once in awhile Bob would run into women, but he really tried to stay clear of them. Women on the road frequently seemed to be a little touched and often bitter about something. He did his best to give them a wide berth. Whenever he had a camp set up, and someone would ask to share it with him he was extremely cautious. He had experienced run-ins with those who tried to steal from him, or those who were non-stop talkers. Often he'd share food and water with people and he had met many who would offer him whatever they had. If they were too far out there in cuckoo land he would just give them his site and move on. Over the years Bob ran into thieves, boozers, druggies, perverts and weirdo's, but most were kind, generous, and often just lonely.

His travels had exposed him to more experiences than he could imagine. Sometimes it was the extremes of weather. More than once he was caught in a major snow storm in late spring or early fall. If he was near a town he would try to find shelter of some kind. If he was a long way from nowhere he would use his plastic sheet and make the best shelter he could. If possible he would build a fire but sometimes the wind or rain would be so bad a fire was out of the question and he would have to wait it out. It was during some of these times that he was able to see the real kindness that some people had, especially in rural America.

Once he was walking on a rural road in Colorado as he did his best to avoid travel on the freeways. It was late March and he was in high country and had been watching the clouds to the west toward the Rockies. They were getting darker and he knew from experience that there was a good chance a storm was coming. When the temperature started to drop he knew that there might be some snow in the storm. He started looking for a place to make camp and a decent shelter before it hit, but he was in wide open country and there was not much to pick from. He kept on walking.

If the wind didn't blow too hard he could walk in rain or snow for as long as it took to find a place to hold up. But if that wind picked up and brought a lot of snow with it, it could get a little tough without shelter. He had been in a white out before, where you couldn't see anything and if he hadn't been fortunate enough to stumble onto an old barn, he probably would have died. He kept an eye on the clouds and was pretty sure he was in for it. By three in the afternoon it was almost dark and the snow was coming down pretty hard. Not long after it started snowing the wind came up. By four he could barely make out the road in front of him. He tried to keep a close watch behind him for any rigs, not so much for a ride but because he knew in these conditions he could easily be run over.

Before it started snowing he could see miles in any direction and he knew he had a long way to go before he would find any trees or buildings for refuge. If it didn't let up pretty soon he was going to have to try his hand at building a snow cave to make it through the storm and survive the night. The snow was already a foot deep on the road and getting difficult to walk in. He was getting ready to give up and dig in when he checked behind him and thought he saw some lights. He watched as they came closer. He got off to the side of the road and a truck that was going real slow stopped about fifteen feet past him. The driver backed up enough so that his headlights were on him and then pulled forward again.

A window rolled down and a gruff voice called out, "You better get in here."

He walked over to the passenger side, threw his pack in the back and got in.

The driver turned on the dome light, extended his hand and said, "My name is Jack Nisbet."

Bob shook his hand and said, "I really appreciate you stopping."

"That storm kind of hit us quick didn't it?"

"I've been watching it all afternoon and figured something was coming. Just couldn't find any place to hold up."

Jack looked at him. "I saw it coming too and would not be in it except I still have some cows that haven't calved yet and I needed to check on them." Jack slowly headed down the road into the storm. He glanced at Bob and said, "Where ya headin'?"

"Arizona."

"Don't mean to be nosey" Jack said, "but where you coming from and why are you way out in this country instead down by the freeway?"

"You're not being nosey, I would ask the same. I am coming from Northern Montana and don't like traveling by the freeways. I like this open country."

"What are your plans for tonight?" Jack asked.

"When you drop me off, I will probably try to find some shelter or make a snow cave and wait out this storm."

"Just like that, make a snow cave and wait it out?"

"Yes sir."

They drove in silence for a few more minutes and then Jack turned his truck on to a barely visible driveway and followed it for about a mile. They came over a ridge and Bob could see lights ahead.

Jack pulled his truck up to a large, two story ranch house and turned off the engine. "You don't need to be out in this storm any more tonight. My wife and I would like to offer you a place to lay your head."

Bob looked at him. "Are you sure your wife won't mind?"

Jack opened his door. "Grab your bag and come on in, she is a heck of lot nicer than I am."

As soon as Jack opened the door he hollered, "Jessica, put your clothes on, we have company."

Bob smiled at this and they walked into a warm kitchen that was filled with the wonderful aromas of home cooking.

The lady at the stove turned. "I am so glad you are back safe; it is coming down pretty hard out there."

"It sure is" Jack said. "Jessica this is...I never caught your name."

"Ma'am my name is Bob, I'm very glad to meet you."

"Please call me Jess," wiping her hands on her apron. "Did you get caught out in this storm?"

"I sure did."

Jack sat down and started to take his boots off and said. "Honey I told him he could lay up here for tonight, is that OK?"

"Of course it is, nobody should be out in this kind of weather. You can take your boots off if you like Bob and would you join us for supper?"

"Your kitchen smells wonderful; if you have enough I would enjoy that."

They had a delicious dinner of roast beef, mashed potatoes, home canned green beans, and a big slice of apple pie with steaming hot coffee. Both Jack and his wife picked up on Bob not being much of a talker, so they carried most of the conversation and didn't pry into his life at all. They figured if he wanted to talk, he would.

After they finished their coffee, Jack said it was getting late and he would show Bob to their spare bedroom and guest bath. "You're welcome to take a bath or shower if you like, and if you get hungry you know where the refrigerator is. I am going to leave at sun up to check on my cattle, it shouldn't take long and when I get back I will give you a ride into to town if you want." Bob said he would really appreciate that and thanked them for the wonderful supper. Bob took a hot shower, which was greatly enjoyed. He always kept clean, but it was usually out of a very cold creek or river.

The next morning when Jack walked out his back

door, his truck had all the snow swept off it and the snow was shoveled away from the back door. Bob was leaning against the truck admiring the mountain range behind the ranch. Jack looked at him in surprise, "I figured you would still be asleep."

"What you and your wife did for me last night was a wonderful gesture of kindness and I will always remember you for it."

Jack looked a little embarrassed, "That's just the way folks are around here. Do you want a ride into town?"

"Well if you don't mind I would like to give you a hand with your cattle, I was raised on a ranch and I know sometimes an extra hand can make things a lot easier."

"You're sure right about that, I used to have my boys for help, but they're both away at college. Jump in; let's go see how they did."

Bob ended up staying three days with the Nisbets. On the second day Bob was helping Jack and they went into town to get some supplies at the local feed store. While Jack was talking to the owner, Bob was just looking around. He noticed a couple of young cowboy types talking to man who looked like he was in his thirties. As he got closer he heard the young men laughing and he realized they were teasing the older man. They were asking him how many girl friends he had and saying that he must be a real lady's man. It was obvious that older man was not real smart and he wasn't enjoying the ribbing at all.

Bob listened a little more and finally said to the young men, "It might be a good idea if you fellas left the man alone."

The two men looked at him with surprised expressions. One of them, with his chest puffed up, started walking toward Bob and said, "You should mind your own business, Mister!"

The owner saw what was going on and stepped in quickly and told Bob, "They didn't mean anything; they were just having a little fun with Jimmy."

Bob looked at the owner and said, "It didn't look to me like Jimmy was having any fun," then he walked over to Jack and said, "I will wait for you by the truck." As he was walking out he looked at the two younger men with a glare that said if you want to carry this farther, come on out. They didn't.

Jack came out a few minutes later and said, "I'm going to back the truck up to the loading dock at the end of the building."

After he backed up to the dock, Jimmy came out and said, "What you getting today Mr. Nisbet?"

"Just a couple sacks of oats for the horses and ten bales of bedding straw Jimmy."

After they finished loading, Jimmy walked over to Bob and put his hand out and said, "My name is Jimmy."

Bob took his hand and said, "I am real glad to meet you Jimmy, my name is Bob."

As Bob was walking toward the truck, Jimmy said, "Thank you for sticking up for me, no one has done that for a long time."

"You keep your head up Jimmy."

They pulled away with Jimmy watching them from the dock. Bob expected Jack to question him about confronting the two men, but all he said was, "Jimmy's brother was killed in a car accident a few years ago and I think he has kind of been on his own ever since. His brother took good care of him and no one bothered either one of them. Pete has given him enough work to keep him going but he has been around for so long that people just seem to not pay attention to him much."

"Do you know where he lives?"

Jack scratched his head. "I think he rents a little old house on the west side of town, not sure though."

For those three days Bob helped Jack with several things that can hardly get done by one man. Both men had developed a strong respect for each other and a friendship of the kind that last. While Bob was finishing his breakfast on the last day with the Nisbets, Jack slipped two one hundred dollar bills into his pack and figured it well worth it. When they got in to town, Jack turned off the truck and put his hand out. "Bob you are always welcome at our home and we really would appreciate it if you would stop and see us if you pass through this country ever again."

Bob shook his hand and thanked him and said he would.

When Jack got home his wife asked him, "Why was there an envelope on the bed Bob used with two hundred dollar bills in it?"

After Jack and Bob said their good-byes, Bob walked over to the feed store to see if Jimmy was there. As soon as he came around a corner he could see Jimmy sweeping the dock. Jimmy saw him coming and jumped down and half ran to greet him. "Hey Bob, what are you doing here?"

"Well, Jimmy, I thought I would come and say goodbye to you before I left town."

Jimmy looking a little sad said, "You don't live here?"

"No, Jimmy, I am just passing through."

"Dang... Bob I was hoping we could be friends," Jimmy mumbled.

"We can be friends, I'll be back through these parts again, how about I buy you lunch today before I take off?"

Jimmy, with a big smile on his face said, "That would be great Bob, no one has ever bought me lunch before and I get off at noon today."

"It is a deal then, where do you want to have lunch?"

Without hesitation, Jimmy said, "Right across the street. Henry has the best cheeseburgers in town, bar none."

Bob smiled," I will meet you there at noon."

They had a nice lunch of cheese burgers, French fries, and large Pepsi's. Bob noticed several people giving them the once over more than once and they both ignored them. After Bob paid for their lunch and as they were walking out Jimmy said, "Bob, will you walk with me to my house, I have a gift I want to give you?"

"You don't have to give me anything, Jimmy."

Jimmy with real intensity in his voice said, "I really want to give you something special for being my friend."

"Ok Jimmy, which way?"

Jimmy's house was only a five minute walk in the direction Bob was heading anyway. As soon as they were close enough to see Jimmy's house, he started getting excited. "There it is Bob, do you see it Bob? That's my place, what do think? Do you have a place that nice?"

As they came closer Bob could tell that Jimmy was not much on keeping his place tidy. The lawn was full of tall weeds with lots of junk scattered all over. No neighbors lived close to him so his place kind of stood out like a very sore thumb.

When he got to the door Jimmy opened it without having to unlock it. "Come on in Bob, welcome to my home!"

Before he went into the little house Bob could smell a very strong odor emanating from it. When he got inside the door he was appalled by what he saw and smelled. It had two rooms and they were both totally packed with junk. There was a walkway to a very filthy looking bathroom and another walkway to a bed. It looked like it had been years since he had been close to his kitchen sink, range, and refrigerator. It was also obvious that he had a cat or cats.

Wait right here." Jimmy quickly walked over to his bed and removed a photograph that was thumb tacked to a wall. He brought it back to Bob and said, "This is a picture of me and my brother who was killed a long time ago and I want you to have it and keep it to remember me by, OK Bob?"

Bob took the picture and said, "Thank you Jimmy, I will keep this in my Bible." Looking around the room Bob asked, "Jimmy do you have anyone to help you keep your place picked up a little?"

Jimmy with a look embarrassment said, "I know it's kinda messy, but no one has been in here except you since my brother died three years ago. I just don't know what to do with all of this stuff. A lot of it I find on the street when I'm walking to work or walking home from work. Some of it comes from the boys in town who throw it out their windows onto my place when they are out drinking and driving around. I hear them laughing, but I am afraid to say anything to them. My brother use to take care of all this."

"Tell me, Jimmy, you must have a cat or two in here also?"

"I sure do Bob, four of em. They are kind of wild though, only one will let me pet it."

Bob stepped back outside as he could not take the tremendously strong order any longer. Jimmy, if I got someone to help you with your place would that be all right with you?"

Jimmy with a big grin on his face said, "It sure would! I would love to clean this place up if I only knew how and what to do with all of this stuff."

"What is your work schedule the next few days?"

"I'm off tomorrow and the next day," Jimmy said with pride.

"I will be back in a few hours, don't go anywhere."

Bob walked to a gas station they had passed by on their way to Jimmy's house. He asked the attendant if he knew of a state human services office in town. He told him he was in luck as there was one only a few blocks away and Sally was only there one day a week and this was the day she was in town, as she had three other small communities she served also. Bob followed the attendant's directions and found the little office without any problems. He had previous experiences with case workers for kids in foster programs, seniors, and disabled.

Most of the time they were wonderful people, over worked and under paid. Their caseloads were always way too big and they seemed to get flack from just about everyone. In Bob's book they were a special breed of people who deserved a lot more respect than they received.

When Bob walked into the office, Sally was just getting off the phone and said, "Can I help you?"

"Well ma'am, not me so much but I have a friend that I think can sure use some."

"What is your friend's name?"

"Before I tell you that I need to run something by you first, would that be OK?"

"Shoot, I am all yours for 15 minutes and then I have to meet some foster parents who are having some problems. Will that work?"

"It will. Here's the deal, I've worked with different state programs in the past and have a pretty good idea how they function. My friend is developmentally delayed and I think he has kind of slipped through the cracks. His brother was his caregiver, however he died three years ago and my friend has been living on his own ever since. Now you have to understand that he is carrying his own weight financially as he has a job that he's been successful at for several years. The problem is that his home is very unsanitary and I am afraid it will cause some serious health problems for him in the future. What I don't want to happen is for the state to see the conditions he's living in and panic and want to put him in an institution. What I am asking you to do is allow me to show you the condition of his home in its current state and then look at it again in two days. Give us two days to make it what it can be and then I would like to ask you to put my friend into a program that will help him learn some basic skills that will enable him to do a better job of keeping his place up. Can we go at this problem from this angle, ma'am?"

"We sure can," Sally replied. "Let me call my foster parents and buy a few more minutes and we will go look at your friend's place right now."

"I like the way you do business."

Jimmy, his boss, Pete, Jack and Jessica Nisbet, Bob and two pickup trucks hit Jimmy's place like a whirlwind. The owner of the landfill gave them a discount and they ended up taking nine pickup loads of junk that Jimmy had accumulated over the last three years. Under the supervision of Jessica Nisbet they made everything spic and span after they had hauled all of the garbage away. They talked Jimmy into letting animal control take the cats after Jack offered to give him a pup from his beautiful Austrian shepherd who was due to give birth next month.

Jimmy was very excited about that.

When Sally showed up three days later as planned she almost cried. All of them were there and she looked at them and thanked them from the bottom of her heart. She said, "If communities would do this type of thing for each other more often, there would be a lot less problems in the world."

The six of them talked for a few minutes, all agreeing to help Jimmy keep his place up. Jimmy was grinning from ear to ear and everyone else had a tear or two in their eyes. Bob said his farewells and walked out of town heading south on the same road that caught him in a snow storm the week before.

CHAPTER 2

He was walking along looking for a good place to get a few hundred yards off the road so no one could see his camp fire. He was in the high desert of Arizona and the terrain was hilly with some pine trees, but mainly sage brush and sand. With what light he had left he could see a small grove of trees ahead about a quarter of mile which looked like it would give him some good cover from the two-legged varmints that he had become so leery of. As he got closer he heard voices coming from the trees. He would have to keep on going and distance himself from whoever was there. He noticed that there was a little dirt road that went back into the trees. He passed it by and had gone about fifty yards when he heard the scream of what sounded like a young girl. He figured it was some kids goofing off and having a little fun scaring each other. He went a few more feet and the next scream was obviously not from someone having any fun. He decided to circle around and come in from the upper side of the trees and check the situation out. If someone was in trouble he might be able to help and if they did not need any help they would never know he had been there. The closer he got the more he realized that something was wrong. As soon as he crested a small hill he could see that there were two vehicles with lights on. As he got closer he could see four people standing in front of the lights of one of the rigs, two men or boys and two girls. One young man was struggling with one of the girls and she was trying to hit him and kept yelling at him to leave her alone and let them go. He was calling her names and made the statement that these two girls deserve anything that he decided to do to them and if they didn't start cooperating they might just end up missing... forever. Now the girls were crying and pleading just to be let go and they would never say anything. It was obvious that the boy doing all the talking was Hispanic as he was calling the girls names in Spanish. It was also obvious that they were not complimentary. The decision for him to intervene came when the punk doing all the talking slugged the girl in the stomach and ripped the front of her blouse in the same motion.

They were all extremely shocked when they heard his voice. He did not scream or yell, just showed himself and said, "It would be best for you boys to let the girls go."

After he regained his composure from the interruption of the unexpected visitor, the attacker looked at him and shouted "Who are you and what did you say?"

"I said it would be best for you fellows to move on and let these girls go."

The talker looked at him in disbelief. "What are you talking about you stinking old tramp? You better hurry up and get out of here and we won't kill you!" The talker paused a second as if he was thinking about what he just said and then he looked at the other boy/man with him, who was quit large, and said, "I want you to grab that stupid, tramp gringo and beat him bad enough so that he can't walk and then set him by that tree so he can watch what we are going to do these two. They are going to get exactly what they asked for when they chumped us into buying them beer. They wanted a party and now they're going to get it and no stupid tramp is going to mess it up." He grabbed the girl by her arm and pulled her close to him.

Big boy who had not said a word to this point looked at the talker and said, "Lucky, let's just get out of here. This is not looking good. Come on let's just get out of here!"

Lucky glared at him and said, "No tramp gringo is going mess up this party." Then he screamed at big boy, "Do what I said!"

Big boy started to come toward Bob. Bob put up his hand and said, "Lucky, you do not want to do this."

Lucky screamed at big boy again and the girls and big boy all jumped and big boy came at Bob. He outweighed Bob by over 100 lbs and was at least eight inches taller. Because Bob was so much smaller, he was just going to grab him and smack him around like a rag doll, which Bob was sure Lucky had him do too many others that challenged him. Big boy was his strong arm and it was obvious that he would do whatever he was told. As he was reaching for Bob's collar the first punch that hit him was two knuckles from Bob's left hand to his throat. The next was the palm of his right hand square into his nose. He was in so much pain from both blows that he wanted to swear and scream, but the blow to his throat was causing some breathing problems; he was on his knees with one hand on his throat and the other on his nose just kind of gasping.

This all happened in less than to two seconds and when Lucky realized that big boy was on his knees and the little man was still standing he was shocked and explosive. "You stupid tramp" and at the same time he pulled out a knife saying, "This is the end for you old man!"

As he lunged at Bob with the knife in his right hand, Bob side stepped and grabbed Lucky's wrist with both of his hands and twisted with everything he had. He heard a popping sound and the knife fell on the ground. Lucky's wrist was probably broken and Bob just wanted to get these boys moving down the road in the opposite direction of the girls.

Bob bent down to pick up the knife and throw it in the brush when he heard one of the girls scream, "Look out!"

Bob felt something like a baseball bat hit him in the left side of his head as he was wheeling around to see what she was warning him about. Lucky and big boy were in front of him, who was using his head as a baseball? What he didn't see was that Lucky had two thugs and the other one was relieving himself behind some brush. When Bob showed up he came around behind him with a large tree branch.

Bob was lying in the dirt when the first kick to his kidneys was delivered by Lucky. All he could hear was Lucky screaming at him and kicking him over and over again in the back, stomach and face. The last thing he heard was big boy say, "I am leaving right now," and the man who hit him in the head say, "What about the girls?"

Big boy responded, "They ran off into the brush and I'm not about to go after them."

Lucky, who was completely out of breath growled, "That tramp better be dead and we need to get somewhere to fix the pain in my wrist."

CHAPTER 3

When Bob was able to open the only eye he could see out of, he had no idea where he was or how he got there. He knew better than to over react, so he laid there and tried to put the pieces together. After a minute he realized he was in a hospital. His right arm was strapped down with an IV in it, but he could move his left arm so he reached up and touched the eye that he could not see out of. It was covered with a large bandage and he also felt bandages on his head and his left ear. He did not know what to do; he was in terrible pain just about everywhere on his body, especially in his lower back. Then it all started to come back. Lucky, big boy, the girls and all the blows he received from Lucky's boots. How did he get here? Did the girls bring him, and were they all right? All he knew was how much pain he was in and how much he did not want to be in this hospital. He knew that there would be a massive amount of questions and he did not like answering questions at all. He decided he would put off answering any serious questions for awhile. Maybe they could help him out with the pain and he could get out of here as soon as possible.

She was fussing around with his bedding and the IV and humming a song she probably heard on the radio. She was probably a nurse and had no idea Bob was conscious. When she finally looked at his one eye and saw that it was open, she jumped and let out a little scream.

"Oh my you scared me, why didn't you say something? Can you talk, are you okay, are in you pain, what is your name, what happened to you? Look at me go on. The doctor said he wanted us to contact him as soon as you are awake. I will be right back; don't do anything, like trying to move, OK, promise?" She hurriedly left the room.

In less than two minutes she was back with two other women in the same color uniforms and a short, pudgy, balding man in a doctor's coat. Four sets of eyes staring at Bob's one eye all obviously very curious about their mystery guest. He knew there was going to be an onslaught of questions and before they even started coming he had already decided to milk the fact that he might be a little confused on many things, especially the questions on who he was and what happened.

The doctor took control and said, "First of all, what is your name?"

Bob looked at him, pretending to think and said in a much labored voice, "Bob."

"Bob, my name is Dr. Martin and you are in the hospital in Layton, Utah. Can you tell me if you are in pain and where?"

He looked at him with his one good eye and wanted so much for the terrible pain to ease up a bit. He let out a very wispy, "Yes."

"Do you mean yes, you are in pain?" Bob nodded his head a little and the doctor seemed so happy with all of this communication and said, "Can you tell me where your pain is located?"

Bob was pretty happy with communication also, so far he had gotten away with only saying two words. Bob and yes. He decided to keep this few words thing going. Bob motioned with his free hand for the doctor to bend down and for him to think that it was going to be very difficult for Bob to speak loud enough for him to hear him. He put his little chubby ear close to Bob's mouth and Bob said, "Back and ribs."

"I figured you would have a lot of pain in your abdomen as your back has a considerable amount of bruising and you have four fractured ribs. Are you allergic to any medication?" When Bob shook his head no the doctor immediately told one of the nurses the pain medication he wanted and he became Bob's hero.

She was gone in a flash and must have been anticipating the doc's request, because she was back in a few seconds and injected the medication into Bob's IV line and the extreme pain started to subside. He closed his one open eye and pretended to drift off to sleep.

"Whoa, he is out already," said the doctor. "I was hoping to get some information out of him." He looked at one nurses and said, "Go call the sheriff of Kaibab County and let him know that his mystery man is conscious and it looks like he might make it. Tell him that we will call him as soon as it will be OK for him to talk to this man." He told another nurse the dosage of pain medication he wanted to maintain and to keep a close watch on his urine for blood as he was very concerned about internal bleeding. To the other nurse he gave orders to change the dressings and to be real careful with this poor man's ear.

When Bob realized that they were going to work on his bandages while they thought he was unconscious, it made him a little nervous. He kind of wished he was out of it, because there was probably going to be some serious pain in changing his dressings. On the other hand he was very curious to hear what they would talk about when they thought he could not hear them. He was not a stranger to pain and he would give it his best shot to keep them believing that he was out and if the pain got too bad he would wake up all of sudden to get gentler care.

As soon as the doctor walked out of the room the three nurses started talking. "Who is this strange little man and how did he get beaten so badly and how is he still alive?" one of the nurses said.

The nurse who first saw he was awake said, "He was brought in by ambulance last night to the emergency room. ER did their best to stabilize him and got him into the OR where two surgeons worked on him for over three hours putting his face, eye, and ear back together. He had lost so much blood before the ambulance got to him that everyone was pretty sure he would not make it."

"Did he have any ID on him?" asked another nurse.

"No, from the way he was dressed they figured he was a transient and that another transient had beaten him up for a bottle of booze or something. What they can't figure out is who made the 911 call telling them where to find this guy. They said it sounded like a young girl, but she hung up without giving any further information. It happened over in Arizona and the sheriff of that county is pretty sure that this amounts to something more than a couple of tramps beating each other's brains out for a bottle of cheap wine. Apparently that sheriff is pretty anxious to talk to our Bob here, as soon as possible. They told me he has called three times to see how Bob is doing and asking when he could talk to him. Sparky King, from the *Chronicle* in Elmira, has called a couple times trying to get information also. He overheard something on his police scanner and thinks there might be a story here."

"This is the most excitement we have had in this little hospital in a long time. We better make sure we take very good care of our little friend."

As she was speaking the silent nurse was taking off the last of the bandages that covered most of Bob's head. "Oh my," she exclaimed, "I have never seen anyone beaten this badly. His ear looks like hamburger and you can see all the work they had to do to his eye socket, nose, and cheek bone. His chart says that he has four fractured ribs and possible kidney injuries. Well, let's just do our best to clean him up and change his dressings."

By this time Bob could not take the added pain any longer and decided to come out of his fake slumber. They all jumped when they saw his one good eye open. "That is the second time you have scared me," squealed the nurse who had first discovered him.

"How bad is it?" Bob whispered.

None of them knew what to say, then finally one said, "You don't worry about a thing, we are going to take real good care of you. You will be fine."

"How soon can I get out of here?"

"Your doctor will be talking to you about that Bob. You have some pretty serious injuries so you're going to be with us for a few days. Don't worry about any of that right now."

"Maybe we should let the doctor know he is awake and maybe give that sheriff a call."

When she said this Bob raised his one good hand a little and they stopped and listened as he said, "I would just like a little more of that pain medication that you gave me and I would sure like to get some rest before I have to talk to anyone. Besides, if I have to talk to anyone I would rather talk to you ladies than to anyone else."

Two of them giggled and then one said, "That's OK, Bob, don't you worry about that. We will protect you for a while. We will get you much stronger before they start quizzing you, OK honey?"

Bob thanked her as she was giving him some additional pain medication. It felt so nice for him to really be falling into a deep sleep.

It must have been some time during the night when he woke up. The lights were dim in his room and it was quiet in the hallway outside his open door. A flood of thoughts were going through his head as he lay there in pain. To add to the list of discomforts he was very hungry and really needed to use the bathroom. He hated the thought of having a nurse take care of his business and decided to give it a go on his own. He saw that his IV pole was on wheels and his arm was not strapped to the bed anymore. He was able to pull his covers off with his good hand and started the process of propping himself up enough so he could get the side rail down on his bed and roll out. The pain was excruciating but he kept working at it and when he was just getting his legs over the edge of the bed he heard a bellowing voice say, "What do you think you are doing?"

He looked up at her like a school kid caught smoking and said, "I was just going out for a dinner and a movie and if you're nice you are welcome to join me, but only if you pay your own way."

"Very funny, now get your skinny little butt back in that bed."

"I was not actually asking you out, yet, but could sure use a go at that bathroom."

"That is good news, the doctor is very anxious to get a sample of your stool, I will get a bed pan and fix you right up."

"Ma'am, I think I was less than two years old the last time someone gave me a hand in that area and I would like to keep it that way."

"First of all, my name is not ma'am, it is Alice. I let some of my closer friends call me Sweet Alice, for reasons you will learn to understand soon enough. Until me or that doctor of yours, says otherwise you will use a bed pan." She toned down a skosh and said, "Don't you go getting all manly and embarrassed about getting a little help in this private matter. It will be fine and before long you will have your privacy back."

"Ok Alice, looks like we are going to do things your way. Since you seem so dedicated to taking care of my needs, do you think I could get something to slow this pain a little and maybe a bite to eat."

She finished up the unpleasant task at hand and said, "I will be right back."

She brought back the wonderful needle of relief, and she also carried a binder which she laid on the bed before she injected the medication into his IV. "Usually they put someone with your kind of injuries on a steady dosage of pain medication for a few days, however, your doctor wants you to ask for it so that we might gather a little more information from you. Such as what is your full name, all we have is Bob. Are you going to help me out with that Bob?" Before he could answer she said, "When I came on shift the nurse I was relieving told me that you had made the request for a little time before you had to start answering a lot of questions. Questions like who are you and what happened. Do you know what I mean, Bob?"

Again, before he could say anything she said, "I have been around a long time and when I see people beat up, it's usually because of one of two reasons. One they were low down snakes and they deserved it or they were in the wrong place at the wrong time. Where do you fit in this assumption, Bob?"

He liked Alice, she was straight and he felt he could trust her. She was a large Hispanic woman with no accent. Bob was pretty sure she ran a tight ship, but also sensed a deep compassion that she had for her patients. The night shift was hers and he was sure that she did it well, the way she thought it should be done. He looked at her, and said, "Alice, could I ask you a few questions first."

She looked at him, paused, and then said, "Shoot."

"Can you tell me if there has been any blood in my urine or stool?"

"There hasn't been any in your urine and it did not look like any in the first stool sample. These types of questions are for your doctor and not me."

"Please bear with me. I just feel more comfortable talking to you than a doctor right now."

"Yeah right, you don't want to talk to that Arizona sheriff or Sparky King either, who seems to think that there is a very interesting story behind this mysterious Bob guy."

"Please Alice, just a little more info and I will give some back, OK?"

"All right, what do you want to know?"

"How bad are the ear and eye injuries?"

"In laymen's terms Bob, your ear was almost torn off. The surgeon was able to get it sewn back on and if the bandages are dressed properly and infection does not set in, it will be fine, except for some interesting scars that you can cover with longer hair. The eye on the other hand, we won't know until tomorrow how well they did. Your eye was almost kicked out of its socket, but the real problem was the chipped and fractured bone around the socket. After tomorrow when the doctor checks it he will be able to give you a better idea what you will be dealing with in the future. It might involve more surgery or possibly some loss of vision. Dr. Martin is a good doctor, we just do not see eye to eye on a few things. If you go telling him that I told you this, it is going to cause some problems for me, do you understand?"

"Alice I appreciate you giving me this information and you definitely do not have to worry about me betraying your trust."

"For some reason, Bob, I do trust you."

"Okay, Alice, one last question. Do you know if there was anyone else hurt the night I was or do you know of anyone missing?"

She looked at him for a moment and then said, "You got beat up trying to help someone out didn't you?"

His silence answered her question.

"No, I do not know of any other injured or missing people from that night." When she saw the relief on his face, she said, "Would you do it again after what happened to you?"

Bob just nodded his head a little and looked out the window.

She looked at him, with intensity and then said, "Because of doctors orders I can only give you clear broth and maybe some Jello. I will put in my report that communications with the patient was very limited." Alice smiled at Bob and walked out to get the broth.

CHAPTER 4

Kerry was seventeen and a student at a small high school that bored her to death. Her father had run off when she was only two years old, so she had no memories of him at all and did not have any desire to ever see him. She had built up such a strong resentment toward him that she could not stand the thought of him coming back into her or her mother's lives. Her mother was a nurse at a hospital in Layton, Utah and was Hispanic. She was told that her father was white and that she favored his looks much more than her darker skinned mother. If you did not know that her mother was Hispanic you would never have realized that Kerry was half-Hispanic. Her mother worked the seven to seven night shift, Wednesday thru Saturday and left around six every night and did not get home until after eight each morning.

After Kerry turned 15 she started hanging out with Molly Seymour who was just as bored with life in a small town as Kerry was. Molly lived with both of her parents, plus three brothers. She considered her brothers nothing short of pure idiots. One was younger than her and the other two were older. The two older ones had dropped out of high school, and, from the way things looked, the third would follow suit. Her mother was totally addicted to food and TV. She had gained so much weight that people who had not seen her for a long time did not recognize her. Her father went from one job to another and spent a large portion of his meager paychecks at taverns and on his love interest at any given time. The three boys were always in trouble of some kind and Molly just stayed out of trouble and under the radar and her parents let her do just about anything she wanted. Their main concern was that she did not get pregnant and create one more mouth to feed.

Kerry's mom was a lot more concerned about her only daughter's success and welfare, but working nights and leaving Kerry unsupervised had its risks and Kerry's mom knew it. She called and checked on her regularly and required her to let her know what she was doing at all times. Both Kerry and Molly did pretty good in school because they knew that an education of some kind was going to be what it would take to get them out of this miserable town with its intolerable, idiot teenage boys.

Kerry and Molly were cruising around town in Molly's older brother's beat up pickup truck just as they had many times before. It was easy to convince her brother to let her use his pickup. First, she had so much dirt on him that if she went to the law she could get him sent to prison. He was pretty sure that she wouldn't squeal on him, pretty sure, but the real catalyst was that because of all the babysitting she did, she had cash for gas, which he usually didn't. Besides she took better care of the old truck than he did.

Both girls knew Lucky and his two shadows from high school. They were also seniors, but with little chance of graduating because they were hardly ever at school anymore and in trouble most of the time. They were able to keep their heads above water by either not doing real serious crimes or at least not getting caught at it. They were American born Hispanics who spoke English and Spanish very well.

Lucky considered himself a lady's man and was not at all shy about bragging about it. He especially took pride in bragging about his exploits with white girls. So when they saw Kerry and Molly cruising around town he decided to turn on the charm. Striking out was not a big deal. In Lucky's mind, not trying was just plain stupid. So that is what they did, chase girls all night.

When they pulled up beside the girls and gestured for them to roll down their window, Molly was not surprised or concerned. They had never really hung out with these boys but knew them to be roughnecks, but not that bad of roughnecks. Besides, Lucky was kind of cute.

"What's happening," Lucky hollered at the girls as they continued to drive.

"Not much, "Molly replied, "You?"

"We're bored," Lucky shouted back.

"Too bad, so sad," Molly replied with a sarcastic tone along with a slight smile.

The slight smile is all Lucky needed to pursue this avenue. "Very funny, what are you two doing?"

"We are going to the church to pray for you losers."

Lucky laughed, "You are really on a roll. Instead of you two giving us a bad time, why don't we get a couple beers and talk about graduation."

Molly looked at Kerry, "What do you think?"

"I don't know Molly; we really don't know those guys very well."

Molly shouted at Lucky, "Meet us at the city park in five minutes."

She turned off at the next street and pulled over. Molly looking at Kerry and said, "You're right about not knowing these guys very well, but we are bored to death and I know Lucky can get us some beer. We don't know anyone else who would buy it for us unless we are willing to mess around and you know that leads to a very dead end street."

Having sexual relationships with older boys or men

spelled disaster. They had some friends at school who have gone down that road and it did not turn out well. One ended up pregnant with no clue who the father was and a few others soon realized that they were totally being used and that these guys had no interest in them as people. Not the best way for establishing one's self esteem and once word got out your reputation was pretty much shot.

"I'll tell you what, I will give them enough money to get us a six pack of beer, just for us, and that we are going over to study with a friend and she can't have boys at her house. If they say no, then we pass."

"My mom will kill me if she finds out we are drinking. I don't know Molly."

"Kerry, we are just going to have a few beers, we are not going to get drunk or anything. We will be home in a couple hours. Come on, do this for me."

"Okay, I guess, it might be fun."

Molly squealed and they headed for the park.

When they got to the park, which was only three blocks away, Lucky and his boys were sitting on a bench waiting for them. Molly pulled up by the curb and Lucky walked over to their car like he was the coolest thing that ever lived. "Well what do you two beauties want to do?"

Kerry rolled her eyes and Molly said, "Here's the deal. We are supposed to go over to a friend's tonight and study and she is not allowed to have boys over, so if you would buy us a six pack we would sure appreciate it."

Lucky looked at her second, gritted his jaw a little and then smiled and said, "Sure, why not, what are friends for, right? We are friends, right Molly?"

Molly didn't like his tone and his smile didn't seem

very genuine. Molly took $5.00 out of her purse and said, "Will this cover it?"

Lucky took the five and said, "You bet baby cakes." As he was headed for his car he turned and said, "We'll meet you at The Grove in 30 minutes."

"Why The Grove, why not right here?"

"The cops are watching us too much lately. The Grove it is and if you decide not to come and pick your beer up, we will be happy to drink it for you." With that Lucky turned and was in his car almost pulling away before his two shadows could get in.

Molly turned to Kerry to see her shaking her head. "This has all the potential for turning out bad, Molly. Here, I will give you five buck and let's just pass on this whole thing. The guy gives me the creeps. Did you see the way he looked at you when you said you just wanted the beer?"

"All guys look that way. Everyone knows what they're after, everyone knows that some girls will put out and some won't. We don't and we won't even get out of the car. I will just have him hand us the six pack and we will be gone. Besides, there is almost always someone out at The Grove this time of night. What do say? We can't go through life scared of everything."

"I don't want to go through life being scared of everything, but I also don't want to go through life making stupid mistakes. Sometimes you have to use common sense and what your gut is telling you. Now that I have said that, you big brat, let's go get the beer."

"Now you're talking, let's go have some fun!"

When the girls got to The Grove they found out that no one else was there. Molly did a U-turn and positioned her pick up so that it was headed back out. She looked at Kerry and said, "Don't worry, as soon as they pull up I will ask him to give us the beer and we will be out of here. I will even have the engine running."

"Okay, but I wish I had a big gun right now."

Molly laughed, "You don't even know how use a big gun."

"I know, but I sure would learn fast if that dude starts getting weird. What's the big deal, you just point and pull the trigger right?"

"No there is a little more than that to shooting a gun the right way, but who cares, we don't have a big gun, we don't even have a little knife. I will have this old truck in gear, one foot on the brake and the other on the gas ready to blast out of here if ol' Lucky tries to get lucky. OK? Besides, quit being so negative, you are making me nervous about this whole thing."

The girls saw Lucky and the boys pull off the road and head for them. It was starting to get dark and Lucky had his lights on bright. He was driving kind of fast and slid to a stop right beside the truck. "You made it, smart girls. I thought you might chicken out and we would have to drink your beer."

"Hey Lucky," Molly said, "Thanks for getting us the beer, could we just get it? We're late for our study group."

Lucky looked at her the same way he had earlier and said, "Just hold on there sweet thing, it's in the trunk, I'll pull up here and get it for you. Lucky pulled into The Grove and got out of his car and went to the trunk. He turned to see if Molly got out of her truck and when she didn't he opened the trunk and took out a six pack in a brown paper bag and slowly started walking toward Molly.

Molly was watching him in her side mirror and did not like the vibes this guy was giving off. She looked at Kerry and said quietly, "Roll up your window and lock your door."

She had already locked hers, but she had to leave the window down to receive the beer. Lucky got to her door and she reached out to take the beer and he said, "Whoa baby, what's your hurry?"

"I already told you Lucky, we're late for our study group."

"You know what Molly, I don't think you two are really going to a study group and drink beer with some girl who can't have boys over. I think you two just want your beer and nothing to do some dirty Mexicans. Is that right, Molly?"

"No...that's not right, we just want to get our beer and to go. Are you going to give it to us or not?"

As soon as she said that she let the brake off just enough for the pickup to move a few inches. Lucky cooled his tone a little and said, "Molly, Molly, I was just kidding, here's your beer."

He raised the sack toward her window and when she reached for it he slid his hand right past the sack and turned off the ignition. Fear flooded into Molly like a tidal wave and Kerry was so scared she couldn't speak. Molly tried the ignition to restart the truck but because it was in gear it made no contact. Before she could put it in park and try again, Lucky had unlocked her door and flung it open and pulled her out onto the ground. Immediately Kerry started screaming and Molly got up swinging.

Lucky swung Molly around and held her so she could not strike him and with a great deal of authority said to Kerry, "If you do not want your friend to get hurt, unlock your door and get out."

Kerry knew she didn't have any choice, so she slowly got out of the pick-up. With his hands roaming where they shouldn't, he pulled Molly over to the lights of his car. At the same time he told his boys to get the girl's beer out of their rig and to get Kerry over here, as they were going to have a little discussion on how you treat friends who buy you beer. The smaller of the two shadows said to the other, "You get the beer and the girl; I have to take a leak." They had downed a whole six pack in the last fifteen minutes. Lucky was reading Molly the riot act on how white girls should treat good looking Mexicans who buy them beer. He had already slapped her twice for screaming, but when she started hitting and scratching at his face, he got even angrier, slugged her in the stomach and ripped her blouse in one motion. That is when, to his total disbelief, he heard Bob's voice.

As soon as Lucky started kicking the little man who had tried helping them, Molly grabbed Kerry's arm and took off running into the night. They went about 50 yards and stopped to see if anyone was chasing them. All they could hear was the boys arguing and then their car starting up and peeling out of The Grove and onto the highway. Kerry looked at Molly and said in a very quiet voice, "Do you think they are gone?"

"I don't know, but let's go find out."

"Are you kidding? I am not going back there!"

"Get a grip; those idiots aren't going to hang around after what they were doing to that guy. They probably killed him. We will sneak up there and not go to the truck until we are sure they are gone."

As they approached The Grove all they could hear was an eerie silence. "I think they are gone," Molly whispered, "Let's check on the guy and get out of here."

As they approached him they noticed that he was totally motionless. "I'm going to get a flashlight out of the truck, I'll be right back," Molly said.

"You're not leaving me alone here with this guy!"

"Kerry you have to get a hold of yourself. First of all this guy risked his life for us and he doesn't even know us. For all we know he might be dead, which makes us witnesses to a murder. This whole thing can get real sticky, real fast, so we have to use our heads and not do anything more stupid than we already have. Besides the truck is only 20 feet away."

Molly went to the truck and got the flashlight and when she shined it on Bob they both gasped. "Oh no Molly, I think they killed him!"

Molly kept looking at Bob and Kerry could tell she was fuming. "Those jerks should be put in jail for what they did to this man!" She bent down closer and noticed that he was still breathing. "Oh, thank God, he's still alive," Molly said as she was pulling her cell phone out of pocket.

Kerry looked at her in disbelief, "Who are you calling? You're not calling the police are you Molly? I just want to be away from all of this; can't we just get out of here?"

Molly glared at her and dialed 911. When the operator answered, Molly said, "I am at The Grove five miles south of Elmira on highway 26. There is a man here who has been severely beaten, if you do not get an ambulance here right away, he will die. Did you get that? Five miles south of Elmira in a grove of trees," and she hung up. "Get in the truck Kerry, we are going down the road a ways and pull off to make sure the ambulance comes, and you listen to me," as she stared at Kerry with obvious anger in her eyes and her voice. "I am not sure how this is all going to turn out, but that man definitely kept us from being raped, and he might have saved our lives."

They jumped in the truck and drove about two hundred yards toward town and parked off the road, behind some brush. Kerry had her head in her hands crying and mumbling about how much trouble they were going to be in with the police, her mom, the school, and even Lucky and his boys were going to be after them. After Molly had positioned the truck so they could see traffic and also see if the ambulance found The Grove, she looked at Kerry and said, "I will not leave that man to die, especially after what he did for us. If the ambulance gets there in a few minutes, we will go home and wait till morning. We won't be able to find out anything tonight. But I am telling you if that ambulance doesn't come soon or if it misses the road into The Grove, we are going to do whatever it takes to make sure that man gets help. Do you understand, Kerry?"

Kerry looked up and said, "You're right, I will do whatever you think we should do."

As soon as she said that, they could see the lights of the police and ambulance coming down the road. A police car was in the lead and it was obvious that the driver knew exactly where the road to The Grove was. After the emergency people passed them and pulled into The Grove, Molly pulled her brother's truck out on the highway. Molly looked at Kerry and said, "This is what I want you do. Stay home from school in the morning and when your mom gets home; be up acting all sick and everything. When she gets done fussing over what's wrong with you, ask her how it went at work and if anything exciting happened. Her hospital is by far the closest to here and if he is still alive they will take him there. If he's dead they will probably still take him there. Then, after your mom leaves you alone to your sickness, call me. I am not going to school either. Deal?"

Kerry looked at her with weary eyes and said, "OK."

Molly dropped Kerry off at her home and then she went home herself.

CHAPTER 5

Alice came back into his room with a small bowl of chicken broth and apple juice. "Is that shot I gave you helping ease the pain Bob?"

"I can't tell you how much I appreciate it Alice; it's getting better by the minute. Is that my steak and eggs?"

"Yes it is, but we are out of a good red wine, you will have to do with this vintage apple stuff. Listen Bob, it is almost 3 a.m. and you need to eat this and get as much rest as you can. I believe the doctors have pretty much done all they can for you. From here on out your rehabilitation is going to be up to you using your head, and not doing anything stupid, like getting out of bed before you should. You need lots of rest and for us to keep your dressing changed and injuries clean because right now it looks like your biggest worry is going to be infection. Now your eye is another matter. We will all know more about that in the morning, when the doctor takes off your dressings, and possibly some more x rays. Another area of concern is the possibility of internal bleeding. I think you are going to be okay there because of positive results from your urine and stool tests and the fact that we have not noticed any additional swelling in your abdomen. You listen to the doctors and the nurses and especially me, and you will be all right. I will go now, so you can drink your steak dinner and then get some sleep. Bob, they are labeling you as a transient, but they told me you were clean and I see things like your nails are trimmed and your teeth are well cared for. You don't seem to be like the typical transients we get here. I am not going to bug you now, or any other time in the future, but I would sure like to know what you are all about. I will check on you throughout the night and give you another shot and anything else you might need about 6:30, before everyone starts coming in and I go off shift. Word of advice: If you want a little more time before the doctor, sheriff, and anyone else who wants information, you can tell the doctor in the morning after he examines you that you are feeling pretty rough and would like another day before he opens the gates. OK?"

Bob looked at her with an expression of total gratitude and said, "Thanks Sweet Alice."

She looked deep into his one eye and knew she was dealing with an unusual man.

CHAPTER 6

When Alice unlocked her back door and walked into her kitchen she saw her daughter Kerry sitting at the table with her robe on and drinking orange juice, she immediately said, "What is wrong Kerry, how come you are not in school?"

Kerry looked at her with red eyes that she had rubbed real hard as soon as she heard her mom's car pull up and said, "I don't know Mom, I just feel real lousy. I have a headache, scratchy throat and today there is nothing real important going on in any of my classes and I have all of my books with me so I can study and not get behind."

Alice put the back of her hand on Kerry's forehead, "You feel a little warm. She looked at her real close. Kerry was doing a great job of looking like she did not feel good as she knew her mother could spot fake illness real easy. "All right, but you need to get back in bed and I will check on you before I get some sleep in a couple of hours."

"OK Mom, but could I finish my orange juice first? Why don't you sit down and tell me how your night went."

"Just for a minute and then I want you in bed." Alice knew as an employee of the hospital she was held to strict confidentially, especially when it came to patients. "You know honey, I can't tell you much in detail about our patients, but we did have a little excitement last night."

Kerry, trying not to appear overly interested, looked at her and said, "Oh yeah, what was that?"

"Some of what I am going to tell you is OK because it is public record, it will be in the paper. Before I came on shift last night they brought in a man by ambulance who had been severely beaten. He lost so much blood it is amazing that he lived. Anyway they found him right outside of town at that place where kids hangout, called The Grove. Do you know where I am talking about?"

Kerry looked as nonchalant as possible and said, "Yeah, I think I know where that is."

"Yeah right, I probably don't want to know what you know about that place or what goes on out there."

"Mom I always tell my friends how wise you are."

"You're real funny."

"Anyway Mom, how is he? Is he going to live and do they know who beat him up?"

She looked at her daughter's eyes and wasn't sure whether to be proud of her concern or worried about why she might be concerned and said, "All I know is, the sheriff wants to talk to him, and probably will tomorrow. I think he is going to be all right." Then she added, "I can tell you, honey, but I think this is one exceptional man."

"What do you mean?"

"I can't tell you any more right now, but I will know a lot more after tonight and will let you know if you are still interested tomorrow morning, OK? Now you get in bed." As Kerry was walking out of the kitchen her mom said, "I hope you get to feeling better and I notice your eyes are looking better."

Kerry looked at her knowing how perceptive she was and said, "That is good isn't it?"

Alice sat at the table thinking about her daughter, wondering if she was up to something, hoping it was nothing. Her thoughts soon shifted to the unusual man laying in her hospital and what he was going through this morning.

As soon as Kerry closed the door to her bedroom she started dialing Molly on her cell phone. Molly did not even say hello, "What's the scoop Kerry, did you find out anything? Is he OK?"

"Good morning to you too Molly! Yes, he is alive and he is going to be all right."

Molly sighed, "I am so glad, I don't think I slept all night. Did your mother buy the sick thing?"

"I think so; she didn't make a big deal out of it."

"OK, this is what I want you to do. I want you to get all better before your mom goes to work tonight. Be working on your homework this afternoon and drinking lots of fluids and eating like a horse. When she checks on you for the umpteenth time, you tell her that I called and begged you to go to Layton tonight to see a movie. Do not tell her this, but we are going to pay your mom a surprise visit tonight after the movie."

"What?" Kerry exclaimed. "We can't go see that man."

"Yes we can. One way or the other we are going to thank him and set the record straight. We also need to find out what he is going to tell the police. Almost everyone in this county knows my brother's ugly old pick up and if he describes it to the sheriff, he will be snooping around, thinking that my brothers might be the one's responsible for beating him half to death. This is not kid stuff Kerry, this is attempted murder."

Kerry paused, "Mom did say that he probably won't be talking to the sheriff until tomorrow."

CHAPTER 7

You would think that he was the President of The United States. Only a few minutes after Alice had given him a shot and told him she would see him later, they started coming in. First, all three nurses who had worked on him the day before came in, before their shift even started, to see how he was doing. When he told them he was still feeling pretty rough and sure did not want to get hammered today by everyone, one of the nurses picked right up on that and told him she would make a point to his doctor that he needed another day before all of the questions. He thanked her and she walked out with a very proud look on her face. The mystery man liked talking to her more than anyone else.

The morning was filled with a visit from one of the surgeons, his doctor checking him out, plus x-rays, eye exams, and his dressings changed. A little after noon his doctor came in to tell him pretty much all good news. His vision was going to be fine, just some scaring around his eye, and on his cheek and forehead. His ear was going to be OK if the bandages were changed regularly. His ribs were going to cause a lot of pain for several weeks, but should heal fine if he didn't go banging them up anymore. They could not find any evidence of internal bleeding and the doctor was real pleased about that.

As the doctor was getting ready to leave he said, "We have some administrative paper work that really needs to be taken care of and there are several people who want to get to the bottom of what happened to you." Before he could reply, the doctor continued, "One of your nurses has already put pressure on me to give you one more day before we start pumping you for information. I thought I would wait and see how you are feeling before we go there."

Bob looked at him with all of the pain and sadness he could express on his face and in his eye and said, "Doc I would be forever beholding to you if we could put all of that stuff off until tomorrow morning. I feel real tired and would love for some of this pain to go away."

The doctor studied him, and said, "I guess you are not going anywhere. I will have a nurse give you some more pain medication and we are also going to let you eat some solid food." As he was leaving he said, "I am going to call the sheriff and tell him that he can see you after 8 a.m. tomorrow."

"I appreciate it, Doc."

After the doctor left, Bob thought about some friends he had met in Elmira many years ago. He had been traveling this same route from Montana to southern Arizona almost every year for fifteen years. Ten years ago he was passing through Elmira one fall evening. It was getting dark and he noticed the lights at a high school football field were on. As usual he was in no hurry so he decided to walk over and see what was going on. It was a football game. Having played football in high school himself he decided to find a place with little or no people and watch the game for awhile.

The atmosphere was typical of high school football not unlike thousands of communities across America on a Friday night. The stands for the home team were larger and had a lot more people in them. The high school band was set up in the middle of the home team stands and the cheerleaders were doing their routines on the track that circled the football field. The concession stand at the end of the field was surrounded by a large number of kids from six years old and up. Most of which were running around, talking, laughing, and checking out what everyone else was doing and who was talking to whom.

Bob found a spot on the far end of the field nearest the visitor's side where there were considerably less people. He wasn't afraid of people; he just knew that with the type of clothing he wore and carrying a back pack, just generated concern with some people. He did not blame them for their concern, especially when there wcre so many young children around. He had learned over the years to avoid potential problem areas and this was one of them.

He was just going to watch the game until the end of the third quarter and then disappear into the night. He had only been there a few minutes when he heard a voice behind him say, "Good game isn't it?"

Bob was very good at not letting anyone get close to him without him knowing they were there. He was very surprised that the owner of this voice had gotten so close without him seeing him first. After he turned around to face the voice that dared to sneak into his space, he just stared at a man who was over six feet tall and well over 200 lbs.

When Bob did not answer, the man said again, "Good game isn't it?"

Bob always felt that he could size a person up pretty well by looking into their eyes and listening closely to what came out of their mouth and how they said it. "I just got here, but it looks like a good game."

The stranger said, "Elmira is having one of the best seasons it has had for many years. This game will probably decide who will be the league champs. I'm especially interested because my son is playing."

"Is that right, what number is he?"

"He is number 64, starting varsity guard on both defense and offense, and he is only a sophomore." Then the stranger extended his hand and said, "My name is Juan Salvador."

Bob shook his hand and peered into his eyes and said, "My name is Bob."

"Nice to meet you Bob, are you from this part of the country?"

"No, just passing through and saw you had a game going on. I played when I was in high school and thought I would watch for a few minutes."

"What position did you play?"

"I was an offense end and defense corner back."

"I played the same positions my son does and really enjoyed it. Football was real good for me during those years. I think it probably kept me out of a lot of trouble."

"I know what you mean, what do you do now?"

Bob figured him to be with the school in some capacity and that he was watching the kids running around to make sure there was no smoking, drugs, alcohol, or fighting going on. He saw Bob standing by himself and came over to make sure he was not up to something he shouldn't be. "I am a probation officer for this county and to be frank with you when I saw you standing over here, I thought I would check you out, I hope you're not offended."

Bob looked at him a second and said, "Juan, I appreciate you being honest with me. Like I said, I was only going to watch the game a little while and then be on my way."

"Why don't you watch the whole game?

"I know that people can get a little nervous when a stranger is hanging around, especially when there are so many kids."

"Well I consider myself to be a pretty good judge of character and I'm inviting you to stay and watch the whole game. In fact, I would like to buy you a cup of coffee afterwards, if you are interested. It's not because you are a stranger, it's because I think you might be an interesting person and I would like to get to know you."

"Well Juan, I think you might be an interesting person also and I would love a cup of coffee."

"Great, I'll meet you right here after the game."

Juan walked off saying he better check on a group of kids hanging out by the fence.

Bob and Juan had coffee that evening and Bob ended up staying with Juan and his family for two days. Over the next ten years Bob would stop and see Juan, his wife Mary, their sons Jess and Tino every time he came through Elmira.

CHAPTER 8

Bob made it through the day without anyone bugging him about who he was or what happened at The Grove, but he knew that was going to change in a big way the next morning. He was feeling so much better that he talked a nurse into helping him get out of bed and use the bathroom and walk around the room a little. This caused a lot of pain, but he could tolerate it and he felt he could get well faster the more he moved around.

He had a phone in his room and he asked the nurse if it was all right to use it and when she said it was his phone to use. He then asked her if she wouldn't mind getting him a phone book that would cover the Elmira area. She said no problem, and went and got him one. As soon as she left he was able to find the number for Juan and Mary Salvador.

He dialed their number and on the third ring Mary answered. "Mary this is Bob, how are you?"

"What a surprise Bob, I am doing real well, where are you?"

"Mary, I don't suppose Juan is around is he?"

"No Bob, Juan is in court and won't be home until about six, is there something wrong?"

"Mary, do you trust me?"

"Of course I do, why do you ask?"

"Well, I'm going to ask you and Juan to do me a big favor. I would never ask you to do this but you two are the only people I can turn too."

"Bob you have done so much for us over the years,

you just tell us what we can do and we will be there."

Bob explained a little of what had happened and what he wanted them to do. After he was finished there was a pause then Mary said, "I'm a little concerned about the secrecy part of what you are telling me, but if there is anyone that Juan and I know that we would do just about anything for, it's you Bob."

About 6:30 that evening Alice came into his room to see how he was doing. She was going to be around him all night but the truth was she could not wait to see this guy. He just intrigued her for a reason she was not sure of. "Well, Mr. Bob, how are you doing tonight? Did you survive today without me?" Alice said with a big smile on her face.

"Hi Alice, it is so good to see you, and yes I did well today. The nurses were great, I was even able to get up and walk around, even to the bathroom," he said with a big grin.

"Well don't you get too cocky mister!" Alice said with a stern voice. "Just because you were able to sweet talk those day people, does not mean you will get away with it with me. Understand mister mystery man?" She laughed and said, "I am going to check in." As she was walking out the door she turned and asked, "Do you need anything?"

"It can wait until you have time later."

She looked at him with somewhat of a puzzled look and thought to herself, I wonder what Bob is up to now?

Earlier that afternoon Kerry was successful in talking her mom into letting her go to the movies with

Molly. The turning point in the discussion was when she showed her that not only had she done all of her homework, but she had done extra credit work in two classes. Besides feeling a lot better, there was no school tomorrow.

Molly picked her up around six that evening as the show was to start at seven. Kerry soon found out that Molly had no plans of going to any show. As soon as they pulled away from Kerry's house Molly asked, "Have you seen or talked to Lucky and the boys?"

"No, thank God!"

"I have."

Kerry with an expression of shock and fear in her face and voice said, "Oh no, what happened?"

"Well you know I can see our street from my bedroom window, and twice today Lucky and the boys drove by real slow and the second time, about two hours ago, he almost came to a stop. He revved his engine up and then pealed out right in front of our house. I am pretty sure he found out we were not in school and he is trying to scare me or at least intimidate me, and its working. I realize what that guy is capable of doing and I'm sure that if this came down on him he would be charged with attempted murder, and he knows it. He would get jail time out of this Kerry, and he knows we could put him there. I imagine he also knows that the man did not die, so that's five people who know what he did to that poor guy. He has to be scared, and mad. He probably is blaming us for all of this."

"Molly, what are we going to do?" Kerry said half

hysterically.

"It all depends on our hero, Kerry, and I will tell you all about my thoughts on our way to Layton."

For some reason Bob was sure that the next few hours were going to be pretty interesting, and it did not take long before that started to come true. About 20 minutes after Alice's shift started she came back in to talk to him. "Well Bob, tell me the whole scoop, what did the doctors say, how you are feeling, and what are you going to try talking me out of?"

"Alice I am really concerned whether or not you are having a good day. Is everything all right at home and are you feeling well?"

"Don't be cute, mystery man, or I will make you go back to using the bed pan. Start off with what the doctors said."

"Now Alice I know all of that is in my chart."

"Bob you are the hardest guy I ever met to get the tiniest bit of information from."

"Okay Alice, I am doing much better and I can leave anytime I want. I think I have a whirlpool bath and a massage schedule for tomorrow and then I might just mosey on down the road."

"Mister funny guy tonight are we? I'm sure the doctors are not releasing you tomorrow, but I am glad you are felling better. I'm going to change you dressings; do you want me to give you additional pain medication before I do?"

"No, I want to be fully aware of what and how you change them, and would you mind getting me a hand held mirror so I can see how you do everything."

Alice got him the mirror without giving him any flack. She was starting to take off the dressings on his head and he asked her, "Would you kind of give me a play by play of what you're doing. What I should pay attention to when I'm doing it myself, and also how long each dressing should stay on."

She did an excellent job of explaining to Bob the do's and don'ts of taking care of his beat up old head. There was some real pain involved in the process, but he was able to bear it and he knew it would get better each day. When she was finished she said, "The hospital will give you some ointment and bandages to last you a few days and I'll show you again how and when to change your dressings."

"You know about the only excitement I get in here is when you are in here chastising me. Would you mind getting me the ointment and bandages for me to look at? That way I can kind of get a feel for how to put them on when I get bored. I would also be able to ask any questions that might arise from that educational and entertaining process."

"Sometimes Bob, I don't know whether you serious, pulling my leg, or up to something. I will get you the bandages, but if you try anything stupid like maybe moseying down the road prematurely. I will find you, tackle you, and tie you up like a steer and put you back in that bed with a big ugly security guard watching you while you use your bed pan."

"Alice, I'm a little disappointed that you think I might leave you before my time. By the way you were right; I was going to ask you a favor."

"Here it comes."

"No, it is no big deal. I know it might come as a surprise to you that I have friends, but I do have a few in this area and two of them want to come and see me tonight. They can't get here until a little later, which will put them past normal visiting hours. I would really like to see them, would you mind letting them in for a few minutes?"

"You are really something, now you want me to go breaking the rules, but you're right, that is no big deal. I don't mind, I just need to know their names."

"How come you need to know their names? I'm sure every visitor that comes to this hospital does not have to give their name, how come my friends do?"

"It is just for security reasons, Bob, we can't have strangers wondering around the hospital after hours. Besides I don't want you to bring any wild women in here. No names, no visitors."

Bob did not want to give out any names, but he was in a corner now, and decided to take the chance. "Their names are Juan and Mary Salvador."

"Juan and Mary Salvador, you're kidding! I have known them for years and they are great people. You have good friends Bob, but to tell you the truth that does not surprise me."

"They are really nice people and they mean a lot to me. Thanks for letting them come in to see me."

"No prob, Bob. I have to go take care of some other patients and will bring you the bandages and ointment later."

"You're the greatest Alice," Bob said, as she was walking out the door.

Alice had finished checking on two of the four other patients she had besides Bob. As she was headed for the third, it took her past the supply cabinet for dressings. She put a few days worth in a bag and dropped it off at her station. As she was headed to check her two other patients, Kerry and Molly came walking up to her. "What a nice surprise," Alice said, as she gave them both a hug. "What are you two doing here? Aren't you supposed to be at the movies?"

"I know, Mom," Kerry said, "But it was a really dumb movie and we have not stopped to see you up here forever. We just wanted to say hi and see if you had time for a break or something."

"Girls, I will not have any time for a break for at least another hour or two. I'm sorry; it is kind of busy right now."

"That's OK, Mom, is there anything we can do to help you? Remember we were both candy stripers at one time."

"I know, but you know hospital rules, but you know what? I would like you to meet someone that I think is interesting. His name is Bob, and he is in 211. Here, take this bag of dressing supplies and a can of apple juice down to him. Tell him you're my daughter, and ask him if he is doing OK, and if he needs anything. I know he is bored and maybe he will tell you more about himself than he has the rest of us."

"Mom, is he the guy you were talking a little bit about this morning?"

"Yes he is, and do not tell him I told you anything about his stay here, OK? Here is the bag and juice, remember, just a few minutes."

As they were walking down the hall, Molly said, "I

can't believe how lucky we are. I had no idea if we were going to be able to sneak in to see him or not. Now your sweet mom just gives us an open door, how cool is that?"

"I am glad you are excited, because I am scared to death."

"What are you scared of? Do you think he is going to jump out of bed and call security? Yelling these two girls are the reason I got beat half to death!"

"I don't know Molly, but if he says 'boo', I will probably go running out the door."

Molly knocked on the opened door, "Mister, we have something for you."

The two girls walked into the room, and stood at the foot of Bob's bed. Bob, without any expression studied their faces, "I am glad you both are all right, how did you find me?"

The girls did not know what to expect, but they sure did not expect him to recognize them and be so calm when he found out who they were. Molly with a very surprised look on her face said, "How did you know it was us? It was almost dark out there."

Bob studied their faces for a few seconds and then extended his hand to Molly and said, "My name is Bob, what's yours?"

Molly, without hesitation, walked over to the side of his bed and shook his hand, "My name is Molly and this is Kerry."

Kerry did not move closer to shake his hand, and Bob could see that she was very nervous. "I'm glad to meet you girls and I'm very happy that you are both OK. But, again how did you know who I was and how to find me? If you were indeed looking for me."

"Oh we were looking for you." Molly said. "We had to find you to thank you for what you did for us and to make sure you are all right. This is the only hospital they would have brought you to, and it just so happens, Alice, your nurse, is Kerry's mom."

"Oh my," Bob exclaimed, "What an interesting coincidence. Well, Kerry I think your mom is one very special person. But, I am pretty sure you know that already."

Kerry, who was still very nervous, mumbled, "Yes I do."

There was a silence and Bob broke the ice by saying: "I would imagine that both you girls, and Lucky and his friends are very interested in what I have told people concerning what happened in that grove of trees the other night."

Molly with a very nervous smiled, said, "Yes sir, you are sure right about that."

"Well let me tell you what I plan to do and what I want you to do, OK?"

"Yes sir," they both said at the same time.

"First of all my name is Bob, not sir."

The girls nodded their heads and started to relax a little. Bob in a very quiet and calm voice said, "I have not talked to anyone about what happened that night and more importantly I don't plan to either, ever, but only if you both agree to the rest of what I have to say."

The girls, with obvious relief on their faces, nodded again. "Here is the deal...the sheriff is going to be here tomorrow morning. I do not plan on telling him or anyone else, anything concerning you two or those boys. If you don't have it already I want you to get a phone number for

Lucky and tell him that, which should ease his mind considerably. Do it tonight, so they don't do something else stupid. Also, I want you to tell them that I will go to the police in an instant, if they do anything to threaten or harm you girls or anyone else in the future. Also, tell them that if the police are unable to do anything to them for whatever reason, I will personally track all three of them down and put their lights out forever. No matter where they go, I will find them, guaranteed. I have a very good friend that I trust completely, that lives in the Elmira area, who I am sure knows all five of you. I will tell him a little about what happened, but not everything. He will be watching all of you and he knows where I will be and how to get a hold of me. That means that all five of you are going to have to get your act together and go down a very straight path. I know you two are capable of doing good, because you had the character to call 911 and save me from bleeding to death in that grove of trees. You also had the courage to come and see me. I admire that and if you maintain that kind of character you will do well in life. Is it a deal?" Bob asked with a warm smile on his face.

Molly half squealed, then bent over and gave him a cautious hug, as she did not want to hurt him, and said, "You are wonderful and I'll never let you down."

There was a silence and both Bob and Molly were looking at Kerry. With tears streaming down her face she said, "I have never looked into such kind, concerned eyes as yours. When my mom said that you were a very special man, she was right." Kerry walked over and gave him a real, very long hug, and said, in a quiet soft voice, "I will never forget you and what you have done for us," and she walked out of the room.

Molly bent down and kissed his forehead and as she was walking out she stopped and said, "I really hope we meet again."

As soon as Kerry walked out she saw her mother coming toward her from the other end of the hall. Oh no, she thought, she is going to see that I have been crying. Then she remembered that the restrooms for this floor were in the opposite direction. She did not want to yell at her mom in the hospital that she was going to the restroom, so she just made a gesture with her hands and went in the other direction.

Seconds later, Molly came out of Bob's room, and almost ran into Alice. She had not been crying, but her eyes said she was close, so she tried to avoid Alice seeing them. "How is Bob doing Molly?"

"Well, he is doing good, I think. He would not talk about himself much."

"Now that does not surprise me at all," said Alice, "I am thinking about trying some torture or something to get him to open up. Maybe you girls loosened him up a little, I will let him rest for awhile then see how forth coming he is tonight."

"Where did Kerry go?"

"I think she went down to the restrooms."

They started slowly walking toward the nursing station and before they got there Kerry joined them. Her eyes looked a lot better, but there were still some signs that she had been crying or was not feeling well. She knew her mom would notice it right away. When she walked up on them she put her left arm over her mom's shoulder and held her mom's right arm with her right hand. By holding her this way, her mom could not look at her directly. "You are right, Mom, that Bob guy is an interesting man. Where do you think he comes from, and where he is going?"

"Don't have a clue sweetie, but my curiosity is getting to me. I hope to know more tonight or at least after everyone drills him tomorrow. I am glad you girls got to meet him."

"We are too, Mom. Molly, are you ready to go? I am kind of tired." Molly said yes and hugged Alice and the two girls started walking down the hallway. Alice watched them, forever concerned for what they were going to do and their safety, but also very proud of both them and how they handled themselves.

CHAPTER 9

The girls headed straight for Elmira and as soon as they had good enough cell reception Molly called a friend that she knew would have Lucky's cell number. Molly pumped herself up and even started to get mad so that she could get over the fear of making this call. Maybe he wouldn't answer and she could do it later. No, Bob was right; this needed to be handled right away.

"Yeah," Lucky answered his cell phone on the third ring, "Who is it?"

Molly thought this guy is so full of himself; he can't even answer the phone without trying to impress someone. "Lucky, this is Molly."

Lucky went right into a tirade saying, "It's a good thing that you called because I was going to start kicking some people around and asking questions later. You, Kerry, and that tramp are on the top of my list."

Molly felt a surge of anger and screamed into the phone, "Lucky, shut up, and listen to me and do not interrupt!" She took a deep breath, "First of all Lucky, you wouldn't kick anyone around, you would hide behind your shadows and have them do the kicking. I think we both know that if you and the tramp, as you call him, where to go toe to toe, even with him beat half to death, he would put you away. So spare me the tough guy stuff. You're nothing but an insecure punk that is not going to do anything. You have two losers to do your dirty work for you. You think you're really something. Well you are not, you could Be something, but right now you're nothing."

"Molly, you are digging a big hole..."

Before he could finish Molly screamed at him again; "No interrupting! I feel better telling you what me, and most other people in this town think of you. Now I'm going to give you some good news. Kerry and I just left the hospital, where we had a nice visit with a very interesting man that you in your stupid, perverted mind call the tramp. I tell you Lucky, that man has more character in his little finger than you will probably ever have. I want you to keep in mind that what you did to that man is called attempted murder. You hearing me, hot shot? Attempted murder! That means many years in the slammer where you really belong. He would have died if the ambulance had not gotten there in time. Then it would have been murder and four people saw you do it. Don't get all tough and puffy with me or we will change our mind and the next visit you get will be from the law. Is this sinking in Lucky boy? A simple yes or no will do."

"What do you mean, change your mind?"

"A simple yes or no is what I said!" Molly screamed at him.

Lucky quietly replied, "Yes."

"Good, I think you are starting to understand with that little brain of yours how deep the doo doo is you are standing in. Here's the deal, and you listen very carefully. You listening?"

"Yeah, yeah, go ahead."

"That man's name is Bob, and this is what he wants to do, and as far as Kerry and I are concerned, what he says, goes, period! The sheriff is going to be knocking on his hospital door tomorrow morning and when he sees how badly he was kicked with your boots; he is going to want to come after whoever did it, real bad. Here's the good news for you sport; he's not going to tell him anything. I don't know how he's going to get away with that, but I am sure he will think of something. For him not spilling the beans on all five of us he has some requirements that all of us have to live up to. Are you still listening?"

"Yes I am, but, it better not involve giving him any money because I don't have any."

"Man, you are really something. He's letting us off the hook and you still are only thinking of yourself. You haven't asked how he's doing or that you are sorry for what you did to him, and what you were planning to do to Kerry and me. What makes you think you have the right to rape teenage girls, and beat a man as bad as you did Bob? Tell me Lucky, what gives you that right?" There was silence, and then Molly screamed as loud as she could, "Tell me!!!"

"All right girl, we were out of line, and things kind of got out of hand. But, if you had not asked us to buy that beer for you and then split, none of this would have happened."

"I know a guy like you is not man enough to stand up and take responsibly for his actions. But I do have to grant you the fact that I need to take some of the blame for this nightmare, and I do. The difference is, I feel really bad for Bob and Kerry and everything that happened and all you can do is think of your own pathetic hide. I'm so sick of talking to you, here is what Bob said. He knows someone very well, that he trusts, who lives in Elmira. This person, whoever it is, knows all five of us. He also knows where Bob will be and how to get a hold of him. He said if you or your shadows threaten or touch one hair on our heads or anyone else's, he will go straight to the sheriff and press attempted murder charges on all three of you. He also said, if for some reason the sheriff will not or cannot do anything about prosecuting you, he we will track you down, no matter where you are or how long it takes, and as he put it, put your lights out forever. I am telling you Lucky, he was very serious, and I have no doubt in my mind that he would do it. So to put it very simply Lucky, he is letting us off the hook and all we have to do is go down a very straight path from here on out. You and your boys need to keep your mouths shut and we can all put this nightmare behind us. If we do our part, the only one who suffers from all of this is the only one who is really innocent. Talk to me Lucky," Molly said in a very subdued voice.

"Well I guess it would be nice to put all of this behind us and I never want to see him or you two again, so never ask me to buy beer for you."

"Like I said Lucky, you're really something, and I don't mean that in a good way. I know you probably won't tell your boys the truth, but make sure you at least tell them to keep their traps shut," and she hung up.

Kerry looked at her and said, "You need to work on your people skills."

CHAPTER 10

After Alice said good bye to the girls in the hospital hallway she stepped into Bob's room. "I was going to let you rest, but I wanted to see how you were doing and what you thought of those two girls?"

"Well Alice, I am feeling pretty good, little tired is all and concerning those two girls; I was impressed with both of them. Why didn't you tell me you had a daughter?"

"Oh I don't know, it just never came up. Did you have a nice conversation with them?"

"Yes we did, and I like both of them. You should be proud."

"I am, but they both seemed a little teary eyed, do you know anything about that?"

"I don't know Alice, maybe seeing someone as beat up as much as I am might have bothered them. I gave up on trying to figure out what makes a women tick a long time ago. Way too complicated for me."

"I think men can do a pretty good job of being complicated as well. For example we have a man in our hospital, who came in a few days ago right at the edge of death. Most of the doctors and nurses who worked on him were pretty sure he wouldn't make it. Well he did and he's talking and making wise cracks and just carrying on. But talking about complicated, we still don't know this man's name, age, social security number, where he lives or is coming from, where he is going, how he got beat so badly, who did it and about fifty other questions we don't have a clue about. Now Bob you tell me who's complicated?"

"Alice, sometimes when I say something simple and

innocent, you turn it upside down and inside out. I thought you knew by now that I'm just a quiet, shy guy and I'll try to let everyone know the answers to all of those questions tomorrow."

"You know I am just curious Bob. You are going to tell your story tomorrow and I won't find out until tomorrow night. It's just not fair, all the day people get first dibs and I have to wait. I'm sorry, I am whining to the patient instead of taking care of the patient. You said you were tired; we need to get it calmed down in here so you can get some rest. What time do you think the Salvador's will be here?"

"They should be here any minute."

"Well, as soon as they get here I will bring them down for a short visit and then you need to get some sleep."

As she was turning to leave Bob said, "Alice, I need to tell you something."

"Sure Bob, go ahead."

"You know I travel around and meet a lot of people, good people, and then I just go on down the road. Sometimes I meet truly exceptional people, the ones who I am proud to know, let alone call a friend. Those kind of friends are not real easy to find, so when I do, I try my best to stop and see them if I get close to where they live in my travels. When I get back in this country, I hope you will let me visit you. By the way, by this time tomorrow you will know more about me than any of those day people."

"I would like it very much if you would visit Kerry and me, anytime. Now get some rest."

Alice had just got through checking on her other patients when she saw Juan and Mary standing at her nursing station. "Hey you two" she said as she was walking up to them.

"Hi Alice," Mary said, "I thought you might be working tonight."

"How are the boys?" Alice asked.

"They are both fine, how is Kerry?"

"She is doing great; in fact she and Molly were just here a little while ago to say hi."

"That was very nice of them," said Juan.

"Well, Bob told me you might be by to see him and I am so glad he has some good friends in this area. He says that you two and the boys are pretty special to him."

"Well it works both ways," Juan said, "And maybe someday we could get together and talk about all that."

"I would like that, come on, I'll take you to his room." As they were walking she said, "It would be best for now if you don't stay too long, and do not to be too shocked when you see him as he is pretty banged up."

When then walked into Bob's room it was evident that Bob was glad to see his old friends. Juan went right to Bob and gave him a hug and then Mary who was not doing to good job at hiding her tears also gave him a hug and asked, "What on earth did they do to you?"

Before he could answer, Alice said, "I will leave you guys alone to talk," and left the room.

"Oh my Bob, they really did a number on you didn't they?" said Juan.

"It is not as bad as it looks. It is so nice to see both of you and before you we go any further, let me a say a few things. I feel really bad for asking you two to come all the way up here, but I didn't have anyone else that I felt I could ask what I'm asking you two to do."

Juan said, "We would have been really hurt if you did not let us know you were here, but I am not sure what you want us to do."

"Were you able to bring some clothes?" Bob said, while looking at Mary.

Mary opened a fairly large purse she was carrying, "I thought that this pair of pants and shirt of Jess's would fit you."

"I'm sure they will be fine, thank you for bringing them. I have shoes in that closet, but my clothes were in pretty bad shape so they asked me if they could throw them away, and I agreed. OK, here is what I am asking; I know you have a lot of questions and I will tell you two, and only you two, what happened, but I would like to do that later. I need you to know for now that I have not done anything illegal or wrong. However, right now I do not want a bunch of people probing into my life. Like I said, earlier, it is not as bad as it looks. I would like you to stay a few more minutes then go say goodbye to Alice, and tell her thanks for letting you visit this late. She will be in here to tuck me in after you leave and then I know she will probably take a coffee break in the back of the nursing station. If you would pull around to the back side of the hospital I will meet you out there in about 15 minutes."

"What... you want us to break you out of the hospital?" Juan asked. "I can care less about the rules right now, but you need medical attention and this is where you should be for a least a few more days."

"Juan, you need to trust me on this, I will be OK. I have bandages and medicine right here in this bag and I know how to take care of all of my scrapes. I really understand your concern and would totally understand if you choose not to give me a ride. But you must also understand, I am leaving tonight, one way or the other."

Juan shook his head and replied, "I have known for years that you are one stubborn hombre, but this really takes the cake." Juan looked at Mary and asked, "Well, are you into breaking someone out of a hospital tonight?"

"I know one thing, Juan, if we asked Bob to do something like this for us, he wouldn't hesitate."

Juan and Mary said their good-byes to Bob and then Alice and headed for their car. "Is this crazy or what," Mary said to Juan.

"It's defiantly crazy...I hope it doesn't back fire on Bob or us. Doesn't make any difference though, we are not going to let him wander around in his condition."

"You have had a busy evening Mr. Bob, how are you doing?" Alice asked.

"Hi Alice, yes it has been a good evening, how has yours been?"

"Very good, everyone on this floor is resting well, no drama, no emergencies, not yet anyway. Are we going to keep it that way, and are you going to get some rest now?"

"I am a little tired, but something is bothering me."

"What's that Bob."

"I am struggling on how I am going to pay for all of the expenses for this little stay with you; I know they really have to be adding up."

"Well Bob, I can't really speak for the hospital but, I

do know that we get people in here all the time who don't have the ability to pay. I also know they have provisions for cases like yours that involve victims of crimes. Since your incident happened in Arizona and they brought you here, they have an interstate agreement of some kind. If I was you I would not worry about it."

"But these expenses are still real and they came about because of me."

"I know what you are saying, but I don't think you should worry yourself about that. I am sure the hospital's administration people have already realized that you probably do not have the means to take care of it, so please do not worry; it will all work out fine."

"Well I guess you have eased mind somewhat, but still, I hate not paying my own way."

"Bob, I hardly know you, but I am sure that in your travels you contribute more than your share to society. It will all even out, if we just do our best and I am pretty sure that it is what you are doing. Now I want you to get some rest, do you need any pain medication?"

"No, I don't think so, but before you go I would like to thank you for everything you have done for me."

"No prob, Bob, it has been my pleasure. Get some rest and I will check on you in a few hours."

After Alice left, Bob slowly slipped out of bed and closed his door, put on his new set of clothes and after checking to make sure the hall was clear, quietly slipped out of the hospital without anyone seeing him.

Alice took a short break, checked on her other patients, did some paper work and then went to check on

Bob before she took a lunch break. When she walked into his room and saw he wasn't in his bed, she figured he was in his bathroom as the door was closed. She knocked on the bathroom door and said, "Are you all right in there Bob?" When she got no response, she asked again and then opened the door to find it empty. "Oh no, where is he?"

She was on her way out of his room to look for him when she saw a piece of paper on his pillow.

To My Dear Alice,

I know that someone like you fully dedicates their life to their work and their family. Kerry is a very special person and she is so lucky to have a mother like you. The patients who come and go through this hospital are also better off for knowing you, as am I. I have done nothing illegal to be avoiding the law, but at this time I do not want my life opened up like a book because of what has happened the last few days. Please understand that my early departure is just something I need to do and that I will be fine and maybe someday we will meet again under different circumstances. Robert Louis Stevenson wrote this and I feel the same way: '*We are all travelers in the wilderness of this world, and the best we find in our travels is an honest friend.*'

Alice, thank you for being my friend.

Forever yours,

Bob

Alice sat on Bob's bed for several minutes looking at the letter. Not normally given to emotions about her patients, she sat there with tears coming down her face and she was not real sure why.

CHAPTER 11

After Bob slid into the back seat of Juan and Mary's car, Juan turned to look at him and said, "Are you sure you want to do this?"

"I'm very sure."

"OK then, where are we going?"

"Do you know that grove of trees and about five miles before you get to your place?" Bob asked.

"Yes I do, is that where we are going?"

"Yes, please."

"Well if you think I am going to leave you there by yourself in your state, you are totally crazy."

"I can lay up there for a few days and I will be ready to move on."

"No way," Mary said. "There is no water there and you will get an infection in no time; not an option! You can stay at our place as long as you want."

"I figured you would say that, but I don't feel good about your boys being exposed to this whole thing. I would really like to see them, but not like this"

Juan replied with, "I understand. I don't blame you, I would feel the same way. You can stay at my folk's cabin on Wolf Creek. It's only a few miles past our place. It's clean and has plenty of water and food and we can check on you every day."

"That would be perfect, you two are really something."

They pulled into the grove of trees and Bob directed Juan to the back of the parking area with his head lights pointed into the trees. "Do you see that trail going up that small hill, Juan?"

"Yes I do."

"I am feeling a little rough right now, Juan, if you have a flash light, would you mind following that trail about 50 yards and you will see a large sage brush on the right side of the trail. On the uphill side of that brush you will hopefully find my backpack."

Exactly one week after Bob was looking for a place to camp for the night near The Grove he was back on the road again. The stay at the cabin was wonderful for him to heal up a little and get his strength back. Juan and Mary fussed over him like he was an invalid. He was fortunate to have such friends.

The day after he arrived at the cabin, Juan stopped on his way home from work to check on him. After a little small talk, Juan told him Alice had called him at his office. She told him there was quite a bit of hubbub after the law and hospital officials found out about his departure during the night. The sheriff got there before she got off her shift and quizzed her about any information she had on this man who'd disappeared. She also said she forgot to mention that Juan and Mary had been by to visit him less than a half hour before the last time she had seen him. She asked Juan if it was good that she forgot to mention their visit. Juan told her that it was very good and he appreciated it. Then she told him she didn't know where Bob went or if he had any help from anyone she might know, but if he did have some help, she would sure appreciate it if those who helped him would keep her up to date on how he was doing. Juan told her he felt the same way and if he heard anything he would sure call her and then he thanked her for being her.

CHAPTER 12

Denton, Arizona was about 100 miles south of Elmira. The population had declined considerably when the local mine decreased its work force by 70% and the new interstate totally bypassed Denton by over 20 miles. That was over 20 years ago, and Denton had settled into being a small desert town held together by a few small businesses, local cattle and sheep ranches, retirees, and die-hards that just did not want to leave. The sense of a tight knit community was very strong. Everyone knew everyone else and the old saying you couldn't do hardly anything of the remotest interest without everyone knowing it, held true. It was not the county seat but one of the county sheriffs deputies lived in Denton and he kept his patrol car in town even when he was off duty. His name was Reilly Slug and with his presence the town kept real quiet, which is just the way people liked it. The town had a tavern with one pool table, and a small general store that carried everything from bread and eggs to barbed wire. A small bank branch, beauty and barber shops, gas station, one insurance agent, one attorney, a gift shop for the occasional tourist driving through, and a café.

The café was called The Denton Diner and it was owned and run by Lily Fields. Lily had worked at the diner ever since she was 16 years old. Bill and Marge Quinn had been the original owners since they opened 30 years before Lily started working for them. It was their dream and they lived it. They were young and both had good jobs in Phoenix, but did not like living in a big city and wanted to raise their kids in a safer environment. That is exactly what they did for 39 years.

Lily liked the way they treated people and the

quality of food and service they provided. She liked the fact that the diner is where so many people would come almost daily to eat, or just have a cup of coffee and shoot the breeze with whoever was there. Lily's parents had both died before she turned 20 and Bill and Marge treated her just like a daughter and she loved them very much.

Two weeks after the 39th anniversary of opening their diner, Bill died of a heart attack. It really shook up the whole community. Bill and Marge had been an intricate part of the lives of just about everyone who lived there. Hardly anyone coming home for a visit would not stop and see them before they left again. They made it a point of remembering everyone's name and had a sign on the wall that said "No one stays a stranger here."

When Bill died it kind of took the wind out of Marge's sails. She would often tell Lily that it just wasn't the same without Bill around. She started leaving Lily in charge more and more often and she would go visit her kids. One day, not long after Lily turned 25 years old, Marge had her sit down after they had closed and told Lily she wanted to sell her the diner. Lily did not know what to say. She knew that Marge would probably sell the diner sooner or later and she figured she would use that for an excuse to go to college, start a career and maybe even meet Mr. Right. She loved the people of this town and she liked working in the diner, but owning it, that was nothing she had ever thought would happen.

Marge said, "Listen Lily, I know that this is probably a surprise to you, but Bill and I talked about it over a year before he died. We both knew that you are more than capable of making a go of this old place and you would treat the folks right. I have talked to all of our kids, and they all said to do anything I want, as they all love you as I do. You would not have to put anything down and I will sell it to you for a real fair price, and you can make monthly payments that will pay it off in 10 years. You don't have to tell me your answer now, take your time and let me know when you have decided."

That night Lily hardly got any sleep thinking about owning her own diner. Marge and Bill were so good at making the diner into an important part of the community, which in turn made it successful. Could she do nearly as well? Would she ever meet Mr. Right in this little town? Would she be able to have a family and run a restaurant at the same time? So many questions, she was having a tough time making up her mind. The next morning she went to work at 11AM and when she walked in Holly Lasiter was sitting at the counter drinking a cup of coffee. Holly was over 70 years old and still ran the cattle ranch that she and her husband had started over 50 years ago. Her husband was killed in an accident riding the range looking for a missing steer. No one ever really knew what happened. They think he was on a dead run when his horse stepped in a hole and broke its leg and when he went down old Ben Lasiter hit his head on a rock and died instantly. Lily really liked Ben but she loved Holly. She was running that big spread with help from two hired hands and had the spirit of a pioneer. Nothing scared her and there was nothing she would back down from, and she would do just about anything for someone in need. Her spread was over 20 miles out of town so she only came in every week or so. When she did come to town she always stopped at the diner. Another thing she always did was show true excitement whenever she saw Lily. She would fuss over her and make sure she was doing all right and always asked her when was she going find a man worth having and start having babies.

After Holly left, Lily looked at Marge and said, "If that offer is still open, I would like to take it."

"That is so wonderful, when did you decide?"

"When I watched Holly Lasiter walk out that door."

As Lily was dabbing tears in her eyes, Marge looked at her and said, "You will do well, I am sure of it. You have what it takes and you are crazy enough to love this kind of place."

The first time Bob stopped at The Denton Diner, Lily had owned it for five years, had been married and divorced and had a two year old little boy named Jacob. Bob had only been on the road for a little over a year, but he felt he had a pretty good idea of a person's character after only knowing them a short period of time. First impressions to him were real important. He had soon realized that people would treat someone who looked even remotely transient different than they would treat someone else. When he walked into The Denton Diner one very nice fall afternoon, fifteen years ago there were only two people setting in a booth drinking coffee. He made his way to the end of the counter and placed his backpack on the floor by his stool. About 30 seconds after he came in a young woman came from the kitchen wiping her hands on a towel. When she saw Bob sitting at the end of the counter she came right over to him, grabbing a coffee pot on her way. He was used to waitresses only saying something like, "What can I do for you, or do you need a menu, or do you want coffee." Some would greet him, most didn't. He remembered their first encounter very well. The first thing this young women said was, "I'm sorry, I did not see you come in. I hope you haven't been waiting long."

"I just came in."

"Good, would you like some coffee and a menu?"

"Just a cup of coffee would be great."

She poured him a cup of coffee and then walked over to check the people in the booth. She went behind the counter and took care of a few chores and then came over to Bob and said, "Please don't hesitate to let me know if you need more coffee or anything else," and then went about keeping busy with waitress stuff behind the counter. After a few minutes she came over with the pot of coffee and gestured with the pot to see if he wanted a refill. When he nodded that he did, she filled his cup and asked him, "Are you from around this area, I haven't seen you before."

When he told her he was just passing through, he expected her to ask where he was headed and after he answered her, the conversation would be over. Instead she asked him a question he would never forget... "Do you like being on the road?" The thing that probably surprised him the most was not the question itself, because he had been asked that many times over the past year. What got his attention was the way she asked it. The tone of her voice, the expression on her face, and her body language all told him that she was genuinely interested in his response and was more than willing to take some time and actually listen to that response. The more Bob watched this charming woman go about her tasks and talk to her patrons, including him, the more enthralled he became. She had a kindness in her speech and manor that he greatly admired. After his third cup of coffee he realized that he was enjoying being in the presence of this delightful waitress who treated everyone with kindness and respect. He decided he was going to ask her something that he would never have thought of doing normally and he was not real sure in his own mind why he was doing so.

When she came over with her ever present smile and coffee pot in her hand, Bob looked her in the eyes and said, "Could I ask you a favor?"

"Sure, go ahead."

Bob felt embarrassed now and wanted to take back his request, but decided to ask anyway. He really didn't have anything to lose. "Would you mind asking the owner of your restaurant if he might have some work that I might possibly do in exchange for a meal? I have money; I am just trying to stretch it out."

She looked at him carefully, not with surprise at his question, more along the lines of his sincerity and honesty. She put out her hand to shake his and said, "My name is Lily and what might yours be?"

"Nice to meet you Lily, my name is Bob."

"Tell me Bob; if I went to the owner of this wonderful establishment, what might I tell that person you are capable of doing?"

Bob was so surprised that she did not turn him down straight away that he was almost tongue tied. He looked her in the eyes, "I can fix or build just about anything. Pretty good with working the ground and don't mind cleaning."

With one hand on her hip and the other rubbing her chin in the state of contemplation, she asked, "Do you have an idea of what would be a fair wage for your labors?"

Bob said without hesitation, "Whatever the owner thinks is fair."

"OK, let me talk to the owner."

"I'd really appreciated that," Bob said expecting her to go into the kitchen or go to the phone.

Instead she just turned to a mirror behind the counter and said to the mirror, "Well do you think we can trust this stranger who drinks a lot of coffee?"

"I don't know, what if he is a lazy no account who might steal you blind."

"That could be, but what if he is honest and does good work."

"You know we have a lot of things that need fixing ever since you ran that no account off six months ago. What say we give him a chance and if he does us wrong we will give old deputy sheriff Reilly Slug a call because he would love to run him off, especially since he has such a crush on you and all."

"Very funny, let's do it, now go back to sleep and keep the wise cracks to yourself."

Lily turned back to Bob and said, "Well the owner is a pretty tough old gal, but she said it was OK. But, if you mess with us, she will call on this mean killer lawman we have roaming around these parts."

He smiled and said, "That sounded more than fair and make sure you thank your boss for me."

"Will do," Lily said as she handed him a menu, "You can have anything you want," and walked away.

Don't you want me to do the work first?"

"Course not, can't expect a man to work on an empty stomach."

Bob ordered the cheapest meal on the menu and enjoyed the first good, hot food he had in several days. After he finished, Lily took him for a tour through and around the diner. She showed him several things that needed attention and asked him which one he might feel comfortable doing. He told her he could take care of any of them if she had some tools. She took him to a room attached to the back of the diner. He was quite surprised on the amount of tools and fix-it things that were in this little shop. She told him that the original owner had accumulated all of that stuff over the years and she inherited it when she bought the place. She said she did not know how to use most of it and her one and only ex-husband didn't either.

"Well Miss Lily, with the tools you have here I should be able to fix just about anything that needs fixin."

"That's good, let's give that drippy sink a go in the restroom and don't call me Miss Lily and I won't call you Miss Bob."

Bob smiled and said "OK," and Lily walked back into the diner.

About fifteen minutes later Bob was back at the end of the counter waiting for her. Lily came over to him and said, "Was that too messed up to fix?"

"No, it's fixed."

She had this questioning look on her face, "You fixed it already?"

"Yes, it just needed a new o ring in the hot water faucet. It was good that you had me fix it, because it was costing you money for it to be running all the time."

"If that doesn't beat anything. My ex said it was too

messed up to fix and I know for a fact if he could have fixed it, it would have taken him hours."

"I was glad to fix it, what's next?"

"Nothing, if I was to have a plumber fix it, it would have cost me a lot more than that hamburger you had."

"I guess I should get going then." As he was picking up his back pack he said, "I notice you have a lot of open land behind your place, would you mind if I go about a quarter of a mile or so out there and camp for the night?"

She told him he was more than welcome to and even gave him directions to a spot she thought he might like. He thanked her for that and the meal and as he was heading toward the door she stopped him and asked, "Would you mind stopping in here in the morning before you leave?"

"I'll be glad to," Bob said and left.

He found the spot she had told him about without any problem and set up a real comfortable camp that he enjoyed, especially when he had a nice little camp fire going and the stars came out.

About nine the next morning Bob walked into the diner and went to the end of counter just as he done the afternoon before. Lily was ringing someone up at the cash register when he came in and after she was finished she came over to him with coffee pot in hand, "Good morning Bob, I thought you left or were sleeping in."

"No I was just waiting for it to slow down a little bit in here. It looked like you have been pretty busy for the last few hours."

"You mean you have been waiting for hours for it to

be not so busy in here?"

"Yes, was that wrong?"

"No, I guess not, but why didn't you just come on in?"

"I figured you wanted to talk to me about something and I didn't want to bother you when you were busy."

"If that don't beat all." She looked at him for a few seconds then said, "I figure you for ham instead of bacon and your eggs over easy and whole wheat toast, is that right?"

"Well ma'am, that is right, but I usually don't have a breakfast like that."

"What kind of breakfast do you usually have?"

"A granola bar and maybe a piece of fruit if I have it."

"Tell me, is that because you don't like ham and eggs or something else?"

"Something else."

"That's what I figured, I will be back in a few minutes, enjoy your coffee." She came back with a big plate of ham and eggs, hash browns, toast, and orange juice. "Don't say anything, just enjoy your breakfast. It's on me as part of the leaky faucet deal. One more thing, not only don't call me Miss Lily, please don't call me ma'am either. After you finish your breakfast I will tell you what I have on my mind."

Bob enjoyed the best breakfast he had had in a long time. After he had finished, Lily filled up his coffee cup and cleared away his dishes. "Here's the deal Bob, I am impressed with you and how you handle yourself. As you saw with our walk around this place yesterday, there are a lot of things that need attention that are not getting it.

When you told me about that leaky faucet in the restroom it got me thinking. Oh well, I will just come out with it. I can't afford much or I would have a lot of these things fixed already, so I guess what I am saying is, I would like for to you consider staying on for awhile and I will feed you good and pay you $50 a week. If we are both happy after a few days then you can make yourself a decent place to sleep in that tool shed if you like. That's it, I know it's not much of an offer, but I would really like you to consider it."

Bob looked at her a few seconds and said, "You might think that is not much of an offer, but I think it is a great offer and would love to take you up on it. I have to tell you though, if it works out for you, I would be heading north before the weather gets real hot down here and if you wanted me to I would be back in the fall."

"Like you said, if it works, that would work for me just fine as my fall and winter months are my busiest." Lily put out her hand and gave Bob a real strong hand shake, "Welcome to Denton."

The first year went very well; he got to know most of the locals and was struggling with leaving when spring rolled around. When he did leave it was obvious that both he and Lily were a little sad about him talking off to God knows where. But he did and neither one of them knew if they would ever see each other again.

When he came back that fall and walked into the diner, looking just as he had five months earlier, Lily ran up to him and gave him a big hug and said, "I am so glad you came back, I have so much to tell you." Bob was embarrassed by the hug and even though he didn't say it, he was very glad to see her as well.

Bob had been back in Denton for about a month and was on one of his long hikes into the mountains. When he got back there was a travel trailer parked next to the tool shed. He figured that Lily was letting someone park it there for awhile. He walked into the diner and as soon as he came in Lily said, "What do you think of that travel trailer in back?"

"It looks like a pretty nice rig, are you storing it for someone?"

"No, it's yours to use if you like."

Bob with a real surprised look on his face said, "That would be wonderful, but where did you get it?"

"I didn't get it, Reilly asked me if I thought you might like it instead of that tool shed and I said let's surprise him because I knew you would like it. If we asked you first you would try talking us out of it. It was all Reilly's idea. He said he never uses it and it would make him feel good if you would get some use out of it."

CHAPTER 13

He remembered those first days like it was yesterday. They were the start of a fifteen year relationship for Bob with Lily and her son Jacob, and almost everyone else that lived in Denton or came through town on a regular basis. He couldn't believe how fast those fifteen years had gone by. He would show up in late September or early October and leave again usually sometime in March. Jacob was now 17 years old and a junior in high school. Lily was in her forty's and had never remarried. She had many suitors, but none she considered takers. Reilly Slug was still the deputy sheriff and still had a crush on Lily. He had married and divorced twice and put on quite a few extra pounds.

Lily had several different people working for her over the years. Some real good people, some not. Last year when Bob was there she lost a real good waitress named Sally Van Dyke to a truck driver who would stop two or three times a week. After Sally left she hired Lucy Slug, Reilly's second wife. Since Reilly came into the diner, often twice a day, it created an atmosphere that could be real interesting. Reilly was not real quick on his feet or with his mind, but he was quite opinionated and it got him into some pretty interesting discussions when Lucy was in ear shot of Reilly's voice. This happened just about all the time as the diner was small and Reilly's voice wasn't. Bob liked both Reilly and Lucy and hoped they were still there when he returned.

Almost every year when he was returning to Denton he would climb a small hill that was about a quarter of a mile outside of town that had a lone juniper tree on it. From there he had an excellent view of the town and more importantly, The Denton Diner. He would just sit there under that tree for awhile and thank God for having this place and these people to return too.

He had been there only a few minutes when he saw a sheriff's patrol car park on the side of the highway below him. Even from over two hundred yards, Bob recognized Reilly Slug getting out of the car and start walking toward him. This was the first time he had ever had this happen and the first thing that came to his mind was what had happened up in Elmira a few weeks prior. By the time Reilly got to where Bob was sitting he was sweating and breathing real hard. Bob stood up and they shook hands and Reilly said, "Its real good to see you Bob."

"It is nice to see you Reilly, did you walk all the way up here to greet me?"

Reilly sat down and was leaning against the tree catching his breath and looking at Bob. "I was heading out of town and I saw someone sitting up here and I figured it might be you. Looks like you had a little run in of some kind from the looks of your ear and cheek there Bob. What happened?"

Bob knew Reilly was snooping around and simply said, "Nothing much, just slipped on a slick rock in a stream a ways back."

"Slipped on a rock, huh? Must have been a pretty mean rock."

"You know how mean some of those rocks can be out there Reilly."

"Well, Bob I have known you for quite a few years and even though I didn't trust you at first I know you to be a real straight shooter. If you slipped on a rock, you slipped on a rock. I did however; get a call a few weeks ago from the sheriff up in Kaibab County. He said a man had been beaten pretty bad up there and was in the hospital up in Layton, Utah. Before he could get any information out of this man regarding who he was and what happened, he slid out of the hospital during the night and no one has seen him since. He said as far he knew this fellar hadn't done anything wrong, but he would sure like to talk to him. He also said that this guy was beat so bad he would have bleed to death if it wasn't for a mysterious 911 phone call from what sounded like a young girl. He asked me to look out for a transient who looked like he had some recent head trauma. Any idea about any of this Bob?"

"I don't know Reilly, sure glad that poor sucker made it. Like I said, there are some pretty mean rocks out there. Just a coincidence that fellar ran into one like I did."

Reilly looked at the ground a few seconds and as he was standing up he said, "That's good enough for me, it's good to see you again, are you heading into town?'

"In a few minutes."

"Well, I will see you later then."

Bob watched him leaving and said, "Thanks Reilly."

Reilly didn't say anything just waved his hand in the air.

Bob walked around the back side of town and came in behind the diner and dropped off his backpack by the travel trailer. He went to the side where a window was by a booth at the end of the diner. There was no one in that booth so he stood there and looked in the window at Lily messing around behind the counter. There were a couple of people he did not recognize sitting at the counter drinking coffee. He just stood there and watched her for several seconds. He was struggling with his emotions as he realized how much she meant to him, when as if she had a second sense, she looked straight at him through the window.

She dropped the towel she was holding and came running out the back door. Over the years Lily would always greet him with a hug and enthusiasm, but this time it was different. She put her arms around him and just held him and he her without either one of them saying a word. Finally she released her grip on him and said, "Look at me," as she took a Kleenex out of her apron and wiped the tears from her eyes, "Just like a school girl or something." When she looked up she saw that Bob's eyes where very wet also and then she saw his cheek and ear and said, "Oh my Bob, what happened to you, who did this?"

He just smiled and said, "Lily I am so glad to see you, I've missed you, how is Jacob?"

"Oh, he is doing great and he is going to be so glad to see you". Then she put her arms around him again for a few seconds and then did something she had never done before, she kissed him on the lips and said, "Come on in, the coffee is hot and you must be starving."

They were walking in the back door of the diner as the couple at the counter was walking out the front door. Lily said, "Thanks, you two. See you later." They waved at her and left.

Bob and Lily were alone in the diner and both of them were nervous. Lily grabbed a coffee pot and poured him a cup and said, "You know Bob you leave me for months on end and then you show back up here looking like you have been in a war, what is the deal with that?" He just smiled and she walked over and put her hand on his face and said, "I guess it doesn't look that bad, it kind of makes you look like a warrior. I know you are a warrior when you're here, are you a warrior when you out there roaming around the country?"

"I don't know about the warrior part, but yes, sometimes you run into things out there. Just part of living, happens to all of us, this time it kind of showed up on my face. Hope I didn't scare you, must look pretty bad."

"No it doesn't look bad, but I bet there was some real pain involved in this one."

"Oh, it wasn't that bad"... and he started to say something and Lily was also going to say something at the same time but the front door opened and in came Lucy Slug.

When Lucy saw Bob, she smiled and walked over and gave him a big hug and said, "Welcome back gentle spirit, I am real glad to see you. I see you have not necessarily kept out of trouble while you were gone. I told you when you left that you should stay here and we would take care of you."

"Hi Lucy, it is so nice to see you. You're looking very good."

"Thank you, Bob. I'm sure you've been asked by everyone that sees you what happened to your old noggin; tell me when you feel like it. I am really glad to see you back; there has been one individual that we both know who has kind of been a pain ever since you left. I am telling you Bob; this one individual I'm talking about was a real bear cat for at least two weeks after you left. I can't figure it out, do you have any idea what I am talking about, Lily?"

"I know one thing Lucy, with the high wages I pay you; you should be working instead of standing around spreading rumors."

"Oh come on Lily, you know this town would dry up and blow away if we couldn't talk about one another. Speaking of talking about the screwballs in this community, has our illustrious officer of the peace come in yet to take one of his several hour long breaks for the day?"

"Not yet, should be in pretty soon, especially when he finds out Bob is back."

"I saw Reilly on my way into town. He is looking good and I was glad to see him. We talked a few minutes and then he got into his car and headed north, said he would be in later."

"You really think he is looking good?" said Lucy.

"Yes I think so, Reilly is a real good man and I appreciate his presence in this town. I'm sure if Reilly didn't live here, there would be a lot more crime and more importantly, there would be a lot more teenagers and adults drinking and driving. When I'm on the road I often think how comfortable that travel trailer out back is going to be. If Reilly didn't need that trailer anymore he could have just sold it and put the money in his pocket, instead he lets me use it. I really appreciate him."

"Yeah, I know he is a good guy," said Lucy, "but he drives me crazy sometimes."

"I thought you were already there before you met Reilly," Lily said with a grin.

"Very funny, but the way I figure, you have to be a little bit touched just to work for someone as stubborn as you, let alone live in this back water town. Reilly just makes me a little more off track."

Everyone laughed and Bob said, "I don't know about the crazy part, but I do know I have met a lot of people over the years and you three are my idea of the best."

They all sat there for a few seconds and then Lily said, "Bob you must be hungry, why don't you store your gear; I have a new dish I want you to try."

"I have been looking forward to that for a long time."

Several people came in over the next few hours who knew Bob. There was the same type of handshakes and hugs that had been going on every time he came back into town for years. It was good to see all of these old friends. People, who over the years had grown to love and respect Bob for who he was. It wasn't always that way. In the beginning the ongoing rumor was that sooner or later this transient who wandered around the country for half of the year would take advantage of Lily some way or his past, whatever that may be, would catch up to him and they would see him carted off to jail. There was a host of other rumors that were only limited to the imagination of those thinking them up. But as the years went by and people saw all the good in this man, and what he did for so many people. The rumors pretty much faded away. Now he was treated like a regular, who just happened to be gone during the summer.

CHAPTER 14

Reilly came in around three, and as soon he came in Lucy said, "I was wondering if someone decided to shoot you or something, where you been?"

"Missed me, didn't you sweetie pie?" Reilly said with a big smile.

"For one thing, hot shot, I am not your sweetie pie, and no, I did not miss you. It has been kind of nice in here without your constant gibberish all the time."

"Well I know you missed me, because the Lord knows I missed you being nice to me and all. There was an accident up the road about ten miles, and it messed traffic up for awhile."

"Any one hurt?"

"No, just old Henry Monroe was driving a little too fast and lost half of his load of hay on a curve. He was banged up a little but refused an ambulance. I swear some of these old timers are more stubborn than a couple of women I know in this place. Is Bob here? I saw him earlier but we didn't talk too much."

"Yes he is, he's out back fussing around. He's has been around the place twice seeing what needs fixing. And by the way, Lily is stubborn, that is a given, but I am not. You just have not been able to tell the difference between being realistic and being stubborn. Someday you will realize that I am almost always right and you're not. Just a fact....Jack."

"Yeah right, you would be doing good to be right half the time I am. I'm going to say hi to Bob, what do say you fix me up with today's special and I'll give you a big tip. All of this serious police work with no lunch has made me real hungry."

"OK, but I hope this big tip is more than your usual twenty five cents."

Reilly was out talking to Bob when Jacob came through the back door. He looked at Bob and Bob stood up and they hugged and told each other how glad they were to see each other. Jacob told Reilly that his food was ready and Lucy said something about not forgetting your wallet like you usually do. Reilly looked at Bob and said, "Do you see what I mean? The woman is just intolerable."

About thirty minutes later Lily came out with a tray that had three tall glasses of iced tea. "Mind if I join you two?"

"Mom, it is so good to have Bob back, even if he is kind of banged up. Did he tell you what happened? He manages to dance around it every time I asked."

Lily looked at Bob as she answered her son, "You know this man pretty well, and he will tell us in his own good time." They made small talk for a few minutes about business at the diner and school and then there was a silence for a minute, but it wasn't uncomfortable. It was more of a reflective time when all three of them seemed to be thinking about what they meant to each other as they gazed at the huge expanse of desert behind the Denton Diner.

It was about 7 PM and Bob was sitting at the end of the counter drinking a cup of coffee. Lily tried to close the diner at eight every night, but she would never turn anyone away who was hungry or needed someone to listen to them for a bit. More often than not the diner was totally empty by eight so she would start getting ready to close around seven. She did as much as she could for the next day and be ready to lock the door at eight and go home. She was open every day except Sunday and most of the time she was there at 5 AM until closing. It was a pretty hard life, but she liked the people and her only real regret was being away from home when Jacob was there by himself. When Bob was there it was totally different. Bob insisted on getting everything ready in the morning. He would have the coffee made, the grill hot, and open the door at six or earlier if anyone came. Lily didn't have to come in till after six and half the time Bob would have already taken orders and started cooking for any early birds who didn't have a lot of time.

In the evenings, if it was slow, he would run her off around seven and if anyone came in that wanted anything he didn't know how to fix, it was too bad. So when Bob was there it knocked at least two hours off of her day. Time she could spend with Jacob or friends. When Bob left in the spring she realized how much those extra hours meant to her. Also when Bob was there, Jacob would come to the diner to hang out more often. They would do all sorts of things together, whether it was Bob helping Jacob with his homework or Jacob helping Bob with a project of some kind. Bob really didn't need help, but he liked Jacob very much and over the years Jacob became pretty good at being able to take care of the diner when Bob was gone. Often they would put on back packs and go hiking or camping in the desert mountains. Never remarrying again bothered Lily when it concerned Jacob. She knew how important having a father figure could be for a boy or girl growing up. Even though Bob wasn't there all the time he did a pretty good job of filling in that void.

CHAPTER 15

About 7:30 PM a pickup came roaring into the parking lot and slid to stop in front of the diner. Luke McCoy and Larry Swift got out and came into the diner like they owned it.

Ten years earlier, when both boys were only 12 years old, they had a run in with Bob. Bob had put up a basketball hoop for Jacob and any other kids who wanted to play on the back side of the parking lot. One day Jacob, who was seven at the time, and three other kids about his age were playing basketball and having a good time. Bob was working on the back door when he saw Luke and Larry come riding in on their bikes. They didn't notice Bob because he was partially concealed by the diner. Bob had seen them in the diner before and they had never caused any real trouble. He noticed that Luke was loud and somewhat abrasive for a 12 year old and that Larry seemed to follow Luke's lead. They got off their bikes and watched the smaller kids play for a few seconds and then just took the ball away and started playing like the little kids were not there. Jacob did not like this and told them so. Luke walked over to him and pushed him to the ground, and said, "Shut up and we will let you watch the pros." Jacob was mad and scared, but he did not cry or even get up, he just sat there. Luke said, "You better move kid or I am going to thump you." Jacob didn't move. Luke shot another basket and turned to throw the ball at Jacob and saw Bob standing right beside him, but it was too late as the ball flew out of his hands. Bob caught the ball before it would have hit Jacob in the head and put it under his arm. The first thing out of Luke's mouth was, "Give me the ball back," in a very arrogant and demanding way, much like a child who is use to getting his own way.

Bob calmly said, "It's not your ball."

"I don't care old man, give it back!"

"This ball belongs to Jacob, the young man you pushed to the ground. Now I don't know if you know this or not, but not only does Jacob own this ball, he and his mom also own this property. So I think, if you want to play with this ball on this court with these boys, you will need to do a few things."

"Like what, old man?"Luke shot back.

"First, you will need to apologize to Jacob for pushing him down and taking the ball away from him. Then you will have to ask these boys if you two can play with them. I'm sure they wouldn't mind sharing if you wouldn't mind playing fair; after all you two are quite a bit bigger.

Luke whose face was red with rage, said, "You have got to be kidding me you old tramp, you are nothing but a beggarman. I would never apologize to these little weasels."

"Well then, I guess you are going to have to leave."

"If we have to leave I am going to tell my dad and he will be down here to smack you around, you beggarman."

"That would be OK, I would like to meet your father."

The boys got on their bikes and as they were leaving, Luke yelled, "You made a big mistake in messing with me, beggarman!"

After they left Jacob stood up and said, "Why did he call you a tramp and a beggarman? You are not beggarman, you never beg for anything."

"I know, he was pretty upset and sometimes people say things to hurt other people when they are upset. You boys don't worry about it and handed Jacob the ball. I expect you boys to share this court with other kids, but if anyone comes in here being mean, I want you to come and tell me or your mom, OK?"

Luke's dad never did come in to smack Bob around, but a week or so later he was in the diner having supper by himself. After he left Bob asked Lily, "I noticed Lucy called that man by his first name, is he a local?"

"Yes, he lives about two mile south with his son Luke. His name in John McCoy and he is the superintendent out at the mine. His wife just up and left him and Luke a couple of years ago and no one has heard from her since. She hated the desert and didn't much care for the people in Denton either. John works a lot of 60 and 70 hour weeks to keep that old mine making a profit so that the owners don't shut it down. It broke his heart when they had to lay off about 70% of the work force several years ago. He does everything he can to keep the jobs going that are left. He is a good man, but not much of socializer and he is having a tough time with his son. The boy pretty much does what he wants and he's only 12 or so."

"Well that explains his son's behavior the other day."

"What do you mean?"

"Oh nothing, he and another boy were being a little pushy is all."

Over the next few years Luke and Larry would

hardly ever come around when Bob was in town. When he was gone and they came into the diner they would have to behave themselves or Lily would run them off. A few times she had to tell Reilly about them pushing things a little too far and he would talk to them and to Luke's dad. Luke and Larry sat at the counter and as soon as Luke saw Bob sitting at the other end of the counter, he said, "Larry do you smell something bad in here? Smells like a tramp to me."

Lily heard this and walked up to Luke and looked him straight in the eyes and said, "You have two seconds to apologize or get out, I never want you to talk like that in here again. If you don't, you are banned from my place for life. Do you understand me Luke McCoy?"

"Come on Lily, why do you stick up for that old beggarman? He ain't nothing but a tramp."

Lily looked at him with fire in her eyes and said, "If you ever grow up, which I doubt you ever will, I would hope for you to be one third of the man he is, now you get out of here right now, or I am calling Reilly and pressing trespassing charges against both of you."

"Come on Larry," Luke said, "I have lost my appetite."

After they left Lily just stood there with her hands on the counter almost shaking. Bob came over to her and led her to a stool and said, "How about a nice cup of tea before you leave."

"Bob, how can you be so calm when people treat you like that? You are the nicest, cleanest man I have ever met and yet people still say things like that. It just makes me furious."

"Lily, there will always be a certain part of any society who will harbor resentment toward other people for whatever reason. It can be the color of their skin, their religion or their social and economic status. I knew a long time ago that if I wanted to live part of my life on the road I would have to learn to live with it, not condone it, just live with it. One of the reasons I'm here right now is the way you treated me the first time I walked in here. Some people live their life with kindness and compassion; some go through life motivated by self interest and hate. Be grateful that you are not the latter, they're not happy people. I know you have taken heat from people for allowing me to be here and I truly regret that, but we all must just do the best we can and you do a real good job of that. Here, drink your tea."

"I know your right, it's just..."

Bob went to the front door and locked it, closed the window blinds, and then went to the juke box by the back door. He put two quarters in and pushed some buttons. He had never done this before and it really surprised Lily when she heard the coins drop in. Bob walked over to where she was sitting, held out his hand and said, "I would sure appreciate it if you would dance with me."

Lily was going to say something like what if someone sees us and gets the wrong idea and then she realized she had been putting Bob in a different social category ever since she had met him. She looked into his warm eyes and said, "I would like that."

As she was getting off the stool the juke box started playing *The Dance* by Garth Brooks. Lily loved this song and she could not believe how much she loved dancing to it with Bob. Their bodies fit together so comfortably and he led her like they had been dancing as a team for years. She started to say something and Bob said, "You don't have to say anything, it's OK."

The song was almost over and she wished she could dance with this man all night. When it finished he just held her and she heard the juke box clinking as another song was going to play, and it did. It was Dolly Pardon singing *I Will Always Love You*. She couldn't hold back anymore and the tears started rolling down her cheeks. She wished this dance would last the rest of their lives. When the music stopped, still holding her, Bob looked into her eyes, and gave her the warmest, most wonderful kiss she'd ever had in her life. He let her go and took out a clean handkerchief and handed it to her. "Lily someday I would like to tell you what you and Jacob mean to me, but for right now I would like you to go home and be with Jacob and get a good night's sleep." He got her purse for her and as she was leaving she gave him a warm kiss good night.

CHAPTER 16

Behind the diner about fifty yards was an old homesteader's cabin that had not been lived in for over fifty years. It only had two rooms and was in pretty bad shape, but the dry desert climate had let it age gracefully. All of the windows had been boarded up and the only door was busted in and lay against a wall. Bob loved this old house because it had a small covered deck on three sides of it. He put an old rocking chair on that deck and would often sit and watch the sun come up or go down or read his Bible.

About 50 yards to the east of this old cabin was a small trailer park that had eight or nine, older single wide trailers. The park had been there for a long time and was kind of run down. Last year Bob was sitting in his rocker watching the sun fade over the desert mountains when he heard a commotion in the park. A man was yelling and then he heard a women pleading with him not to hit her anymore. Bob had a real problem with anyone hurting anyone else, but a man beating a woman was too much for him to ignore.

He walked over to the park fence and saw a man standing over a women lying on the ground. The man grabbed her by the blouse and pulled her up to hit her again and was very surprised when someone took hold of his wrist and put him flat on his back. The man, with fire in his eyes and booze on his breath, jumped up to start taking his anger out on Bob and before he knew it he was on his back again. He started to get up again, this time Bob put him back the on ground with his face in the dirt. With his arm twisted behind him the man was going nowhere. Bob looked at the women and said very calmly,

"Ma'am, please go into your home, I need to have a word with this person for a minute." The women did just as he asked.

The man was cussing and telling Bob he was going to kill him. Bob twisted his arm almost to the point of breaking it and said, "You need to be real quiet right now and I won't break this arm."

"OK, OK... don't break my arm!"

Bob took a little pressure off the arm and said, "Is that your wife you were beating?"

"It is none of your business you...." Before he could start cussing again Bob put the pressure back on the arm, causing so much pain the man could hardly stand it. "OK, yes, she is my wife. What do you want?"

"Why were you beating your wife, tough guy?"

"I work hard and she got all sassy with me because I had a few beers with the boys after work."

"When did you get off work?"

"I don't know, about 3:30 I guess, what difference does that make?"

"Well that was four hours ago, looks like you have had more than a few beers to me."

"So what, get off of me," the man whined as he was in real pain and didn't want this conversation to continue.

"What is your name?"

"Nick."

"Well Nick, my name is Bob and there are some things I just can't stomach and one of them is some big strong guy getting boozed up and coming home and pounding on his wife for just about any reason. When I see something like that it makes me almost lose control. It makes me want to take that big strong wife-beater and beat him so bad he can't even crawl, let alone walk or go to work the next day. Do you know what I mean, Nick? Now I know you have two little kids in your home and that even makes it worse, so here's the deal. I will let you up and never bother you again. On the other hand if you ever abuse that women or those kids and I find out about it, I will put you in the can't crawl let alone walk mode. Nick I'm not just threatening you, I am guaranteeing it. Do you understand?"

"Yes," Nick whimpered.

"Good, now you go over and sit in that lawn chair and you stay there for at least an hour while you sober up. When your wife, who you do not deserve, comes out to see how you are doing, you ask her politely for a cup of coffee. When she brings it, you tell her that this will never, ever happen again."

"OK," Nick mumbled.

Bob let him up and Nick didn't even look him in the eye, he walked straight to the chair rubbing his arm. Bob knocked on the door and when the lady opened it he said, "Ma'am, I think Nick has something to ask you." Bob walked back to the old shack and finished watching the sunset, listening very carefully for anymore commotion.

It had been over six months since the incident with Nick. Bob had prayed often that Nick had turned his life around and was no longer abusing his family. That night Bob slept in Reilly's travel trailer for the first time in several months and it confirmed in his mind how much he loved the people of Denton and how comfortable he was being part of their lives.

Before Lily left the night before he told her she should sleep in and he would take care of everything in the morning, and she told him she would take him up on that. When Lily got to the diner a little after 6 the next morning she walked into see all of her early morning regulars talking to Bob. It was just like old times, and she loved it. It was busy that morning and they didn't have a chance to talk. Around eight Bob said he was going to go check out the old homesteader's shack. Lily knew he loved being out there reading his Bible or just gazing at the mountains.

He was sitting in his comfortable rocking chair when he heard some noise in the bushes about 20 feet from the porch. He knew it was Nick and his wife's two little kids. Their names were Lura and Joe. Lura was four and Joe was two. Almost every morning that Bob would hang out on the porch, these two little kids would sneak behind that bush. After the incident the previous spring, Nick told the children they could not hang out with Bob on the porch. Instead, they began hiding behind the bush. He had not seen Lura and Joe for several months and was glad to see they still wanted to play their little game. When Bob heard them he would say something like... "Oh no... I think I hear a big old bear in the bushes, I hope it doesn't eat me." The kids would giggle and they would growl and giggle some more. They would play these little word games until Bob would go back to the diner saying something like, "I better get out of here before that old bear gets me." As soon as he was near the diner they would run into the old house and play. Bob had put a little table and two chairs in the shack, complete with a toy tea set and some toys for them to play with.

Before the kids came over he heard a pickup coming

down the dirt road that ran up to mountains behind the diner. He could tell it was coming pretty fast because of the dust cloud it was leaving behind it. When it got closer he recognized Luke McCoy's red pickup. As they went by Luke stuck his arm out the window and pointed his finger at Bob like it was a gun and faked pulling the trigger. Bob just watched them barrel by and shook his head. They'd probably been drinking all night. He hoped they were going to go sleep it off instead of continuing to drive.

Luke said to Larry, "I am going to get that old tramp."

"What are you talking about?"

Luke pulled over to the side of the road and said, "I don't know, I just want to cause him some grief."

"Why do you have a thing for Bob, he has never done you any harm?"

"That bum crossed me several years ago and I don't forget people who cross me," Luke snapped.

"Come on Luke, let's go get some sleep, there's a dance up in Elmira tonight."

Luke just sat there and then took the last swallow out of a fifth of whisky, then he said, "It looks like a great day for nice little bon-fire."

"I don't know what you are talking about, but I know already I don't like it."

"Don't worry about it ol' Larry boy, we are just going to clean up some trash." He got out of the pickup, and from a gas can he carried in the back, he filled the whisky bottle about ¾ full of gas. He then took off his tee shirt and ripped a long strip from it. He folded it a few times and then stuffed part of it into the bottle and got back into the pickup. He headed back for the diner with the bottle in his hand and a mean drunk look on his face.

"I don't like this, Luke, whatever you got planned, just forget it. This is not going to be good."

"Shut up Larry or I'm going to kick you out."

Larry pretty much always went along with whatever Luke said, but this time it was different. "You don't have to kick me out, you just stop this truck and I will get out."

Luke slammed on the brakes and Larry got out. As Luke was pulling away Larry yelled, "Don't do this."

Luke went around the diner and headed up the road toward the mountains. After he was about 100 yards past the old shack he turned around and turned off the engine. He rummaged around and found a can of beer. He opened the can and lit a cigarette. He smoked the cigarette about half way down and started his truck up and slowly pulled up to where he was only 30 feet from the old shack. He stepped out of his truck, lit the homemade wick on the whisky bottle, and threw a perfect strike right through the open door of the old shack. As soon as the bottle hit the floor it shattered. There was a large flash as the gas ignited. The old dry shack became engulfed with fire immediately. Luke jumped back into his truck and headed home with a big grin on his face. "Teach that old bum to mess with me," he said to himself.

Bob was sitting at the counter when he saw Luke's truck go through the diner's parking lot. he thought it odd that he was going through the parking lot again after going through earlier. Something was wrong and Bob decided to check behind the diner just in case. As soon as he opened the back door he saw that the old shack was in flames, he turned to Lily and said, "The shack is on fire, call 911!" Bob had a horrible feeling go through him that shook him to the core. Could it be possible that Lura and Joe were in there? Bob ran into the travel trailer and grabbed the biggest towel he had, dunked in the toilet and went running toward the shack. The fire was so loud he could not tell if the kids were inside. He knew he only had seconds before the fire totally consumed that old building. He put the wet towel over him like a cape and crawled through the flames toward the place where the kids played. When he got close he could hear them crying. There was so much smoke it was impossible to see, but Bob knew exactly where to go. The kids were hiding under the little table. Bob went right to them and turned over on his back.

"Lura get on my chest, we are going for a ride out of here." Lura climbed onto his chest and Bob grabbed Joe's arm and pulled him on top of Lura and covered them both with the wet towel. The doorway was only ten feet away but the smoke and flames totally took away any visibility or breathable air.

Bob started pushing himself on his back with his feet and one arm as he was holding the kids on with the other arm. He got close to the doorway and thought they would make it when something tore into his back. A huge splinter in the old wood floor lodged into his back and stopped him cold. He grabbed Lura under her arms and pushed her and Joe over his head with all of the energy he had left, and yelled, "Run!" Lura could see light and got on her knees and always protective of little Joe, dragged him off the porch onto the dirt.

They were both choking from the smoke and were about 15 feet from the porch when Lily came running to them and pulled them farther away from the fire. At the same time Reilly pulled up in his patrol car and jumped out and came running to Lily. Lily looked at him with more fear than he had ever seen in anyone's face and said, "I think Bob is still in there."

Reilly ran to as close as he could and he saw the towel burning on what looked like it could be Bob's head. Without hesitation he crawled into the fire and grabbed Bob by the collar and literally ripped him out on top of himself onto the ground. Bob was motionless, so Reilly dragged him away from the fire and immediately started to give him mouth to mouth resuscitation. After about 30 seconds, which seemed like several minutes, Bob started gasping for air and coughing. While Reilly was working on getting breathe back into Bob, Lily was using her apron to put out the fire that was burning his pants and shirt.

When Bob started breathing, Lily broke down and started weeping and hugging him. You are never going to leave me again you crazy wonderful man. Bob, still trying to get air in his lungs, was able to say, "What about the kids, are they safe?"

"They're fine Bob; they don't have any burns on them, just some smoke inhalation. They will be fine."

Several people were present now and Reilly told one of the men to help him get Bob in his patrol car and for Lily to get in the back seat and hold his head. Reilly said the ambulance was at least fifteen minutes away and they were going to meet it. They had no time to waste. Over the years Reilly had seen his share of fires and what they could do to someone caught in them. He knew there was no time to spare in getting Bob to an ambulance with a respirator. As soon as they pulled out on to the highway with lights and siren blaring, Bob looked up at Lily, and with his hand, he gently pulled her head down so he could whisper into her ear. "I want you to do something for me," he said weakly.

"Anything, anything at all Bob," she replied as she was sobbing.

"You tell Jacob how much I love him and his mom, will you do that for me?"

"You are not going anywhere Bob, do you understand me. You are going to be OK! Do you understand? You can't leave me. Bob, you can't leave me!"

Bob put his finger on her lips, "You tell Luke everything will be OK if he will turn his life around and look for the good in people." Lily had no idea what he was talking about, but before she could say anything, Bob said, "In my Bible there's a piece of paper with the phone number of Annie York on it. She is my friend and attorney. She will have some instructions for you. Please call her right away, OK?"

"Don't talk Bob, you are going to be fine, you just hang in there." She pulled him as close as she could without hurting him and they just held each other. Five minutes later Reilly said, "There is the ambulance," and pulled off the road to transfer Bob.

The ambulance crew worked as hard as they could to revive Bob, but it was too late.

CHAPTER 17

Lily stumbled into the desert and wept like she had never wept before. Anger built up in her and she wanted to hate God and everything else in her life. The pain was so bad she could hardly stand it. She knew Bob loved her and Jacob and she had just realized the day before how much she loved him. She had fallen asleep the night before dreaming of making a life with this amazing man and now it was all gone. It wasn't fair. Then she heard a red tailed hawk screech above her. Bob loved to watch hawks and often would sit and watch them gliding in the desert sky. Then it became so clear to her, all she had to do was ask herself, what would Bob do? She knew he would want her to be strong and be there for Jacob and to go forward with her life.

She walked back to the men waiting for her and asked the ambulance crew if they would take Bob to the undertakers. She asked Reilly if he would take her home and tell Lucy and everyone else what had happened. "Tell Lucy to put a sign on the door saying the diner is closed and why. I want to be home when Jacob gets there." She couldn't look Reilly in the face because he had been crying and she knew if she looked at him she would start crying again.

Lily walked into her quiet, empty house and was proud of herself for having this desire to be strong for Bob and Jacob. She wanted to crawl into a hole and wish for the pain to go away, but she couldn't. She had to do what Bob had asked her to do, call this Annie York. Bob's Bible, she didn't have it. She called the diner and Lucy answered right away obviously crying and said, "Denton Diner."

"Lucy this is Lily, please tell everyone that I am taking care of everything and will let everyone know what we are doing in the morning, OK, Lucy? We have to be strong for Bob."

Lucy, still sobbing, said, "OK, there are at least fifty people moping around. I will tell them."

"Please ask Reilly if he would go into his travel trailer and get Bob's Bible and drop it off to me as soon as he can."

Ten minutes later Reilly knocked on her door with Bob's Bible in hand. It was obvious he was still pretty shaken up as he handed it to her, "Lily is there anything I can do for you, anything?"

"No Reilly, thank you very much."

"OK, if you're sure, I better get going. There is a lot to do with the fire marshal, who's on his way, as is the county medical examiner."

As he was walking away, Lily stopped him and hugged him. "Not many men would have gone into that fire and pulled someone out."

"I know one thing Lily, Bob would have."

Lily opened Bob's Bible and found a pocket in the cover that had several 3x5 cards with names and dates on them, along with some pictures. One photo was of a teenage boy she didn't recognize. Another was of two men with the name Jimmy printed on the back. The third photo was a picture of Bob and Jacob that must have been taken well over ten years ago.

On one of the cards was the name Annie York and a phone number. She dialed the number and on the second ring a woman answered, "York and York, can I help you?"

"My name is Lily Fields and I am calling from Denton, Arizona, could I please talk to Annie York?"

"One moment please," the woman said and put her on hold.

"Annie I have a Lily Fields from Denton, Arizona on line two, do you want to take it?"

A bolt of fear flashed through Annie like she had seen a ghost for she knew who Lily Fields was and why she might be calling. After a brief pause she said, "Yes, I will take it. Hello Miss Fields, this is Annie York."

"You don't know me, Miss York, but I have something I think I'm supposed to talk to you about and please call me Lily."

"I do know of you Lily, and please call me Annie. I have known about you for a long time and because you are calling me I am terribly afraid that you might have some very bad news for me."

Lily took a deep breath and said, "Am I assuming correctly that you are Bob's friend and attorney?"

"Yes, that correct."

"Annie... Bob died this morning."

Both women could hear the other sobbing and then Annie said, "Lily could I please call you back in a few minutes."

Lily knew she could use a few minutes to get her composure back also and gave Annie her number and said, "Call me as soon as you are ready."

A few minutes later Annie called back and said, "I'm sorry, Bob meant at lot to me."

"That is quite all right, he meant a lot to me and a lot

other folks around here also. Annie I was holding Bob in my arms just before he passed away and the last thing he told me was that I needed to call you right away because you would have some instructions for me."

"That is correct Lily, but could you tell me what happened first?"

"Yes, of course. There was an old building that caught on fire somehow and for some reason, Bob must have known that two little kids were in that building." Lily was trying so hard to keep from sobbing then she said, "Annie, Bob died saving those kids lives."

There was a pause from both women and then Annie said, "Bob left the following instructions in the event anything ever happened to him. First, do you know a Patricia Wilson in Lone Tree, Montana?"

"No, I don't, but Bob had told me he spent his summers in Lone Tree. I have a card with her name and phone number on it and a picture of a woman with a young girl who looks like it might be her daughter."

"That's probably Pat and her daughter Samantha. Bob called her Sammy. You and Jacob and Pat and Sammy were everything to Bob. This may be a little confusing to you; you see Bob would call me on my birthday in July, and the day after Christmas. He never missed a call in fifteen years and someday I will tell you what he meant to me. Anyway, the last time I talked to him, he told me that Pat had gotten married and that he was very happy for her and Sammy. He was always telling me what wonderful women you and Pat are and when Pat married this man that Bob really liked, he was genuinely happy for her. He also said it might be a sign for him to settle down in one place. You might know more about that than I do."

"You are going to make me start crying again."

"I'm so sorry; let me continue with his instructions. First, Bob had a savings account in a bank right there in Denton. As of July he had a little over $12,000 dollars in that account. His instructions were for the money to be turned over to you, to be used for the following. He wanted the most economical funeral service possible, no casket or any of the frilly stuff. He wanted to be cremated and his ashes spread to the wind somewhere. Second, he wanted you to take as much money as you need for you to get Lucy to watch the diner for you, is Lucy still with you?"

"Yes she is."

"That is good, Bob liked her being there with you and someone named Reilly. Anyway he wanted you to take as much money as you need so that you and Jacob could travel to Montana and spend some time with Pat and Sammy. With the remaining money Bob wanted you to use it as an education fund for Jacob and Sammy. He said the fund was to be administered totally under your discretion, something like a $1,000 a year for each of them until it was used up. He felt bad that it didn't amount to much, but he hoped it would help them. Then, finally, he said that he wanted you to know how much he appreciated how kind you had been to him over the years and that you and Jacob meant a great deal to him. Bob didn't tell me this, but I know he was a veteran and if you would like, I will contact the VA and they will help with funeral expenses. They might want to have an honor guard at his service if it would be acceptable to you."

"He never told me he was in the military, it would a wonderful tribute for them to be present at his service."

"Have you thought about when you will have his

service?

"Well, today is Wednesday, so probably Saturday. Do you think that would be all right? What about other people who knew him, like Pat and Sammy and do you know if he had any family? He would never talk to me about his family."

Annie paused for a second then said, "Yes he has a son, who is now married and has two kids. He also told me that if anything did happen to him, he didn't want anyone spending a lot of money just to come and watch him be planted, as he put it. That was pretty important to him. I guess those that we get a hold of can decide that for themselves. What do you think?"

Lily thought a second, "If Bob felt that way, then it was important that everyone knew it. Do you feel OK contacting his son and the people in Montana?"

"Yes I will do that. Tell me Lily, do you think you will drive up to Montana?"

"Yes, without a doubt. What do you think about Jacob and me swinging over to Oregon to see you and possibly Bob's son?"

"That would be a very good idea. It's time for his son to find out who his dad really was."

"You know, Annie, Bob was such a joy in our lives for a long time, but I hardly know anything about his past. I think you probably know more than just about anyone. I am looking forward to spending some time with you so you can help us fill in some of the gaps."

"It would be my pleasure to tell you all I know about Bob. If you let me know when you are going to be here, I will make sure I have as much time as you need and I suggest we meet before you see his son and family."

"That sounds very good to me; I'll let you know our schedule as soon as I figure it out. I must tell you Annie, I feel so much better after talking to you and I am really looking forward to meeting you."

"Me too Lily, call me anytime for anything."

Annie sat at her desk for a few minutes and then told her secretary to cancel all of her appointments for the rest of the day. She went home and grieved for the loss of a dear friend.

Lily sat staring at the wall, wondering what to do next as she waited for Jacob to come home from school. She noticed at the top of a shelf she had by her desk a stack of notebooks. She always kept extras for Jacob in case he needed them for school. She got up and got three of them and sat them before her and just looked at them. Then she said to herself out loud, "Bob why did you want me to drive all the way to Montana to meet this other women in your life?" She opened Bob's Bible and started looking closer at what he had put in the cover pockets. There were the pictures, which she looked at for a long time. She studied the picture of Pat and Sammy the longest. Who was this woman? At first, she felt anger toward Pat for taking Bob away from her for half the year. But was that a true and fair feeling to harbor? Then she thought....was she possibly angry at this women because this man, who opened and closed the diner for her so she could get more sleep and spend more time with her son, would leave and go spend time helping this other women. Then she felt jealousy. Did he like Pat more than her? Did he dream of leaving for Montana when he was in Arizona? Did he regret leaving Montana to go to Arizona? All of these negative thoughts were rushing through her mind. Then she said out loud to herself... "Stop!"

She realized that she needed to be thinking about Bob and what he did for her, Jacob, and the whole town of Denton. He no doubt was the same person in Lone Tree as he was here. The going back and forth thing was something that just happened. He was probably just waiting for her or Pat to find the right guy and get married and he would probably have faded out of the picture. It fact Annie York did say he was very happy that Pat married a good man and that he might be settling down. She vowed to herself to never go down that road of self pity and second guessing Bob.

The bottom line was that she never looked at him as a soul mate. She looked at him as a good guy that was easy to be around and a tremendous amount of help around the diner. She also realized that if she had looked at him differently, with her heart and her eyes, things might have gone in a whole different direction. Bob always said that a person's eyes tell volumes. Her eyes had been telling Bob for years, I love you as a friend and a helper and a transient. What did she expect from a man like him? Even if he loved her and Jacob with all of his heart and would have married her in a heartbeat, he would never go there, because of what her eyes had been telling him for years. She missed the boat, he was gone physically, but not in her heart.

She took the rest of the cards and pieces of paper out of the Bible. There was Pat's name and address on one, the next had the name of Jack and Jess and Bolt, Colorado. Below that were the names Jimmy and Sally. She had never heard of Bolt, Colorado. The next card had Elmira at the top and then Juan, Mary, Jess, & Tino. Under those names, was the name Lucky. Below that was the name Alice, Kerry, & Molly. The next card had Rock River, Utah at the top and the names of Lat and Kate. She found other pieces of paper with names on them but no town or city. She got out a map and found the location of the towns she did have and they were all kind of in a line from Denton, Arizona to Lone Tree, Montana. She thought to herself, I am going to find these people and start putting the pieces together of the other life of the man she truly loved and was to dumb to realize it until it was too late. Even though Bob might not approve, she was going to share that life with his son and anyone else that would let her. She opened up the first notebook and began writing everything she could think of, starting fifteen years ago.

CHAPTER 18

Lily's phone rang all afternoon with people calling to say how sorry they were and to see if there was anything they could do. From the way people talked she realized everyone else saw what was there between Bob and her. Why was she so unaware of it? When Jacob got home he was not surprised to see her there as Bob or Lucy would often talk her into being there when he got home, especially when it was slow at the diner. When he saw her eyes he could tell right away something was not right. When she told him what had happened he hugged her and they both cried for the longest time.

Finally she said, "Bob would want us to be strong for each other."

"I know, but it isn't fair. Bob was good to everyone, why is he gone? Mom, I didn't realize how much I loved him until now."

The phone rang, "Let me get this and then I want to talk to you about something." After she got off the phone she told him about her plan for the two of them taking a trip to Montana and Oregon and how she would work out something with his school.

Jacob mustered a smile and said, "I would like that very much."

Lucy called around six that evening, "I wanted to see how you are doing and to see if you wanted me to open the diner in the morning?

"I have been thinking about that and at first I was going to close it until Monday. But I have decided to open Thursday and Friday. People need a place to come and talk and our place is the best in the county for that."

"You're right, I will be there."

"One other thing, Lucy, I'd like you to consider running the diner for me for awhile as Jacob and I would like to take a little trip."

"I don't have to think about it, you know I would be glad to for as long as you need. I will get my sister to help if I need it and you know Reilly is always hanging around, maybe I will make him wash some dishes or something."

Lily laughed and said, "That will be the day and thank you Lucy for being such a good friend, I'll see you tomorrow."

The two days were a whirlwind of sadness, anger, and reflection from most of the people who came into the diner. The toughest part was when someone would come in who had not yet heard what had happened. Lily and Lucy were amazed how many people thought the world of Bob. A lot of folks cried in that diner those two days.

Thursday afternoon she got a call from Annie York telling her that the U. S. Army would be getting in touch with her. "It seems," she said, "That our Bob was somewhat of a hero and they want to talk to you about the service."

"I'm finding out things every day about him and his interactions with other people that I had no clue about. By the way, Annie, I think my son, Jacob, and I are leaving next Monday to follow Bob's path from Denton to Lone Tree. There are some folks along the way we are going to try to find and after we leave Montana we will head for Oregon and be there in about 10 or 12 days from this coming Monday."

"That sounds real good Lily; I am looking forward to hearing what you find out."

The military thing got Lily curious about Bob's belongings, so she told Lucy that she was going to take a look at Bob's things in the travel trailer. She had been in the little trailer several times and knew Bob wasn't much for possessions. He had added a few kitchen items and a picture of a cowboy with a quote printed on the bottom of it. A pair of binoculars that they had given him for Christmas several years ago, and that was about it. She looked in the little closet and found two shirts and two pair of jeans hanging up. She was about to close the closet door when she saw the edge of a small wooden box. She took the box out and sat down at the kitchen table. When she opened it she saw a passport, which had never been used, a social security card and drivers license. Robert Louis Dolan was his full name. She hadn't known his last name until she'd known him for several years. At the bottom of the box were some military ribbons and medals. She didn't know what they represented and figured she would ask the army about them if they came to his service. She sat there looking out the window toward the desert and realized that this man who gave so much too so many people could fit everything he owned into a back pack.

About twenty minutes later the diner phone rang and it was Captain Marshall Conners from the Army. He asked Lily some questions to confirm that they were talking about the same Robert L. Dolan and then said, "If it was all right they would provide an honor guard for his service." She told him that it would be very nice and the service would be held on Saturday at 11 AM at the only diner in Denton. She was glad that they were going to be there because of Jacob. She knew Jacob and his friends would think that having an honor guard present would be pretty special.

As soon as she got off the phone a thought came to her mind. She got the phone book out and dialed the business number for the county sheriff. She told the lady who answered who she was and asked if the sheriff was in. "This is Hank Sway, can I help you?"

"Sheriff this is Lily Fields from the diner in Denton, how are you?"

"I'm fine Lily. Sorry about Bob, I only met him a few times, but Reilly said he was a real good man."

"Yes he was, sheriff, and Reilly is the reason I'm calling. I want to know if Reilly told you the whole story about the fire."

"I don't know what you mean about the whole story. I don't think he held back any information."

"I guess what I am getting at is did he tell you how Bob got out of the building?"

No, he didn't, he just put in his report that after successful resuscitation Bob was put into his patrol car, along with you, and transported east to meet the ambulance. Why do you ask?"

"I had a hunch that he might have accidently withheld a few facts. You see Bob was unable to get out the house after he got the kids out. He was lying in that burning building totally unconscious. As soon as Reilly saw what looked like Bob's head he crawled into that fire and pulled Bob out. The fire was real intense and I don't know too many people who would have done what Reilly did. He did not hesitate to go into that fire and pull Bob out. I think he should be commended."

"Well I do too, Lily, and I guarantee his actions will not go unnoticed. I really appreciate you calling. These officers put their lives on the line every day and when they go above and beyond their duties I want the public to know about it. Thank you again."

"Thank you, Hank, for keeping Reilly over here in the west side of the county, he really makes a difference."

"I know he does a good job over there and I appreciate you saying so, and Lily, I am truly sorry about Bob."

The phone kept on ringing. People expressed their condolences and wanted to know about the funeral service. They also started getting calls from the press. A Sparky King from Elmira wanted to come to the service and possibly to do an interview with Lily afterward. Two TV stations and three radio stations called about the same. She even got a call from Readers Digest on doing a story. The whole thing had kind of turned into a nightmare, but Lily was grateful for all of the concern and all of the commotion kept her so busy she didn't have time to sit around being sad. By the time she went to bed late Friday night, she was exhausted and fell asleep much easier than she had the night before.

When Bill Quinn died several years before they knew they would have a large community turn out so they had the funeral service right in the parking lot of the diner. Lily had decided to do the same. Bob had told Annie he didn't want a bunch of frills and Lily was holding to that. She had his body cremated and had his ashes placed in his wooded box. The box was positioned on a stand in front of the make shift lectern they had set up for the service. A pastor from a small church twenty miles west of Denton did an excellent job of presiding over the service. He had only met Bob a few times over the years, but knew him well enough to know he was a Christian and shared that and the plan of salvation.

When he opened the service up for anyone who wanted to say a few words; he had no problem getting people to come forward and share something about their relationship with Bob. It was amazing how many people would share a story that no one else knew about. The last person to get up and talk was Reilly Slug.

Many had never seen Reilly dressed in anything but his uniform, so some didn't even recognize him at first. Reilly stood behind the lectern and was silent for a moment. He was obviously working really hard to control his emotions. He finally said, "I'm sorry, this is not easy for me. When Bob first came to town and started working for Lily, I was very suspicious of him and told him so. Instead of being defensive Bob just said he was glad that I kept an eye on someone like him, it showed that I was doing my job. It didn't take long for me to realize what this man was made of. He was honest, kind, hard working and he would do anything for anybody. One of the things that impressed me the most was that he never looked for something in return for his kindness. He would do all of this stuff for people and never mention it to anyone. He did it to help, not to get pats on the back. To give you an idea of what people thought of him, one morning, about eight, I pulled into the diner for a cup of coffee. Bob was up on the roof of the diner peeling off asphalt shingles. I asked him if he was going to redo the whole roof and he said he was. I asked how long it would take."

"I don't know," he said, "A week or two, I guess."

"In this little town it doesn't take long for exciting news like this to spread. I guess that tells us how exciting our town is. Anyway by ten o'clock that morning there were seven men on that roof helping Bob. By one in the afternoon there were 12 guys up there just having a good ole time and by 11 the next morning it was done. I found out later that Bob paid for most of the material for that job. He just made this community stronger by his presence and the way he lived. I can't tell you how many times he would sit with me, drink his coffee, and just listen. He never felt like he had to come across with a bunch of wisdom, he would just listen and encourage. Bob didn't have to talk to impress people. Bob impressed people by his actions."

Reilly paused and asked Lucy to come and stand beside him. "When Bob got back into town a few days ago I was talking to him out behind the diner. I just said that Bob was a listener, well this time I asked for his advice on a very personal and important matter to me. I am not going to tell you what he said. But I will tell you the results of our conversation. As most of you know, Lucy and I were married for a time, and what most of you also know, I was not the best husband around. Well that has all changed and for reasons I am not real sure of, Lucy has agreed to give me another chance. We are getting married one month from today."

A lot of people cheered and clapped and Reilly finished with: "I asked Lucy this morning and she said yes, so today is a day of very mixed emotions. I am elated about being able to start over with Lucy and I am very sad to say goodbye to a very good friend. We are saying goodbye, but this man will not be forgotten."

Then, just as if it had been planned the pastor nodded to the military honor guard and they performed a three gun salute and Taps was played. The pastor announced that at seven that evening Lily and Jacob were going to walk up the mountain behind the diner and spread Bob's ashes to the wind and anyone who wanted to come were welcomed. He also said that the diner would be serving coffee and iced tea the rest of the afternoon if anyone wanted to stay.

Lily was so impressed with the outpouring of the human spirit so prevalent that beautiful fall afternoon in the desert of Arizona. The atmosphere was thick with sadness from the loss of a friend, but there was also a sense of the positive side of the way people feel when they experience the emotions of such a loss. By reflecting on Bob and the way he lived it sparked a desire in people to want to be kinder and more compassionate toward each other. It caused people to examine their existence and what others thought of them as individuals. This self examination of their own character created a desire to do a little better job in the way they treated each other. It also created a strong sense of community. When something like this happens in a community, it causes a person to realize how important that community is, whether it is in the desert of Arizona or Manhattan. Lily always knew this to a degree, but she now fully realized how vital it was for society as a whole. She wanted her son to understand that. She wanted to make sure that she did her part in making her little community of Denton as strong as possible, for the rest of her life.

The first person to approach Lily was Sparky King from the newspaper in Elmira and right behind him were several radio and newspaper reporters. It had all the making of a press conference and Lily was not prepared to be talking about Bob and what he meant to her and this little town. Reilly saw the fear in her face and placed himself between her and Sparky King and said to her, "Do you want to do this right now?"

She was just about ready to start crying and hugged Reilly and said, "I can't do this Reilly, I can't answer these questions right now. But these people came along ways so that they could let other people know about what happened and who Bob was." Reilly took control... He had Lily sit down in a booth with Lucy and Jacob and then told all of the press to follow him outside and he would do his best to answer all of their questions.

When Lily and Jacob came back to the diner a little before seven that evening there were about fifteen of Bob's closest friends milling around and waiting to join them for the walk up the mountain to spread Bob's ashes. To her surprise Luke McCoy was there as well. He was standing by himself by the corner of the diner. Lily greeted everyone and then went over and said hello to Luke. She had forgotten all about what Bob had told her to tell Luke. "Luke, I was holding Bob in my arms before he died and he was only able to tell me a few things; one of them was a message to give to you. I don't know what he meant by this but maybe it will make sense to you. He told me to tell you that everything will work out for you if you start looking for the good in people. Does that make any sense to you Luke?"

Luke looked at her for a few seconds and with tears running down his cheeks, he said, "Yes Lily, it makes a lot of sense to me. I need to apologize to you for the way I treated Bob. If you ever need anything, please let me know." With somewhat of a puzzled look on her face, Lily said she would and thanked him for being there.

As they all were getting ready to start walking toward the mountain, Lily saw Nick and his wife with Lura and Joe walking toward them. She didn't know them very well, as neither Nick nor his wife came into the diner very often. Lura handed Lily a little bouquet of wild flowers, but couldn't say anything. Nick's wife gave her a hug and said how sorry she was. Then Nick, with the saddest look she had ever seen on a man's face, shook her hand and said, "You know that man saved my babies lives, well he did something else for our family that no one will probably ever know. For the rest of my days I will be grateful to him."

As they walked away Lily realized that there were going to be a lot of Bob's life that only God Himself would ever know and understand.

CHAPTER 19

It was Sunday afternoon and Jacob and Lily were rushing around packing a few bags for their trip to Lone Tree. They had never done anything like this before. The diner provided them with a comfortable living, but they could never afford to hire someone to run the place for more than a few days. In the process of packing they realized how eager they were to be going on this journey. At first after Lily told Annie York that they would go to Lone Tree to see Pat and Sammy, she started having doubts. She asked herself why she was putting Jacob and herself through all of this, and then she remembered that Bob had a reason for asking her to take the time to go see this women and her daughter. Whatever that reason was, she was now excited about meeting some of the other people in Bob's life.

Lily and Jacob pulled into the parking lot of the diner at 6:30 the next morning and were greeted by all of the regulars who were there. Reilly was sitting at the counter and they joined him. Lily put her arm around his shoulder and said, "I am so grateful to you for bailing me out with all of the reporters."

"It was no problem, I was to glad to do it."

"Do you know anything about that Sparky King from Elmira?"

"Yeah I know him, why do you ask?"

She explained the card with some people's names on it from Elmira and that she thought her and Jacob would try and locate some of them. But because she only had their first names she was hoping this newspaper man might know them.

"Well, all I can tell you," Reilly said, "is that he has been a reporter up there for a long time. Every time something exciting happened down here, Sparky would come down and do a story on it. He seems to be a pretty good guy, a little nosy sometimes, but I guess a reporter has to be that way to do his job."

"Kind of like a police officer, hey? Lucy said with a twinkle in her eye.

"Are you saying I am nosy, my dear?"

"What is that old saying, something like if the shoe fits or something like that?"

"Well, I can tell you one thing, if I was half as nosy as some of the women in this place..."

Before he could finish, Lily looked at Jacob, and said, "Nothing has changed in here too much, upcoming wedding or not. It's time for us to head north young man."

"I'm with you Mom, let's do it."

Lucy grabbed both of Lily's hands and with all sincerity, said to her, "Take this time and make the best of it and do not to worry about anything here. Everything will be fine."

"That's right Lily," Reilly said, "I will keep an eye on her for you."

Lily replied with, "Believe it or not Reilly; it does make me feel a lot better knowing you are here."

Lucy said, "Well I'm glad you feel that way, I'm not all that sure I do," and then she smiled at Reilly, "I'm glad you're here too... most of time, anyway."

Everyone hugged and Lily and Jacob started their journey to Montana.

Two hours later they were parked in front of Elmira's newspaper office. It wasn't open yet so they waited in the car and studied a map. After a few minutes they saw Sparky King walking down the sidewalk. Lily got out of her car and when he saw her, he thought he recognized her and said "Aren't you the lady from Denton?"

"Yes, I am and I was hoping we could talk to you for a few minutes."

"Of course, come on in."

He was apologetic about the paper not being open and the mess inside, saying something about the gal who really ran things around here had been sick the last few days.

"My name is Lily Fields and this is my son Jacob."

"Sparky King, glad to meet both of you. Come on into my office, I'll grab another chair."

After everyone was seating, Sparky said, "What can I do for you?"

Lily took the 3 X 5 card out of her purse and told him where it came from and handed it to him. "Is there any chance you might know who these people might be?"

Sparky studied the names and paused a few seconds, as if he was thinking about something, and then he said, "Do you think Mr. Dolan knew these people?"

That was the first time she had ever heard anyone call Bob, Mr. Dolan. "Please call him Bob, I'm not use to him being called Mr. Dolan. All I know is that this card and a few others were in his Bible, he never mentioned them to us."

"Well, I think I know who all of these people are. This is a pretty small town and I know just about everyone here. To tell you the truth, though, I am a little confused. Do you mind if we talk about this a few minutes?"

Not at all, that's why we're here, to try and fill in some of the blanks on Bob's past. If these people were close to him, then we wanted to let them know what has happened."

Sparky was rubbing his chin then he said, "After the service Saturday, Reilly told us a little about Mr. Dolan, I mean Bob, not too much though. I think he just told us enough to get us out of his hair. One of things that kind of stuck in my mind was that he said Bob spent his summers in Montana. When he said this I asked how he got from Montana to Denton. Reilly said he walked and hitchhiked and had been doing it for about 15 years. Then I asked him when he got to Denton this year and he told us he had just got there the day before the fire. Is that about right, Lily, is it OK if I call you Lily?"

"Yes, of course it is, and yes that is exactly right. Does it make any difference?"

"One more question, you know reporters, always asking questions. Did Bob have any signs of injuries when he got to Denton?"

Lily studied Sparky's face for a few seconds. This man knew something about Bob that she didn't and her immediate feeling was to distrust him for that.

Jacob started to say something.

Lily put her hand on his arm and he remained quiet.

Lily said, "Could you tell me why you're interested if he had any injuries?"

"Sure, I have nothing to hide, it's mainly curiosity. You see, when you showed me this card, things started to click. You have the names of Juan, Mary, Jess and Tino. That has to be the Salvador's. I know there are no other families with the same four names. I know Juan real well. He's a probation officer for the county and a real good one. Good boys too, involved in a lot of sports. I have no idea why he would know them. Then under their names is the name of Lucky. I only know one Lucky around here and he's a Hispanic kid in high school. Don't know him very well at all; do know he tends to get in trouble once in awhile. No idea why Bob would know him either."

Lily listened in silence.

"Now the next names are the ones that got me thinking. There is an Alice that lives here in Elmira and works as a nurse at the hospital in Layton, Utah. She has a daughter named Kerry and I am pretty sure Kerry's best friend's name is Molly. The reason that perked my interest is that a few weeks ago, a man, who they thought was a transient, was found at a place called The Grove about five miles south of town. In fact, if you came from Denton this morning, you went right by it."

Lily nodded. She'd noticed the area when they passed. Thinking it seemed like the type of place Bob would select, she'd wondered if he'd ever stayed there.

"Anyway, they found a man in that grove of trees because the 911 people got a call from what sounded like a young girl and it's a good thing she called because he surely would have died if the ambulance had not gotten there when it did. This man had been severally beaten, and the most noticeable of his injuries were around his ear and eye. They took him to the hospital in Layton, thinking he would probably not make it because he had lost so much blood. He did make it though and his night nurse's name was Alice. You see, what makes this story so interesting is that this man was in the hospital for three days and on the third night, he disappeared. They never were able to get any information out of him before he left except for his first name and that was Bob. Now you see why I was asking so many questions, the pieces just kind of fit, don't you think?"

Lily looked at him for a second and said; "Only one problem, my Bob had no injuries to his eyes or ears."

Sparky immediately looked at Jacob and noticed as plain as day the confused look on his face. Lily saw him look and knew he knew, but she was going to get some more facts before ol' Sparky got his scoop. Sparky looked at her and decided to drop it. He didn't know how close she was to this Bob guy, but he did know if she wanted to keep a secret concerning Bob it was fine with him. Any man who would give up his life to save others deserved that.

"OK," he said, "Juan is probably at work at the court house and Mary is a stay-at-home mom. Alice works nights and is probably still awake as she most likely just got home. Juan would be my best guess on finding out Lucky's role in all of this and Alice on the two girls. I will be finishing my report on the accident this morning, but it will not be out until Friday. Unless they've seen coverage from one of the TV channels they probably don't know anything about it. I know Alice pretty well, I could call her, if you like, and maybe you could go over there right now."

"That would work out real well, thank you."

Sparky looked up Alice's number and dialed it. It rang several times with no answer and then the answering machine picked up, so Sparky left his name and number. "Do you want me to try Juan?"

"Please."

A receptionist answered and told Sparky that Juan would be out of the office until 3. "Well we're not doing too well here," Sparky said. "I don't know what your schedule is, but if you have time to wait, I could line up something with Alice and Juan after three. In fact, we have a conference room in back that you could use to meet all of them at the same time if you would like. I won't tell them anything, just that a friend of a man named Bob would like to talk to them and we will leave you alone as long you want. By the way I will not dig into this any further unless you ask me to. The strongest rumor going around town, on the mystery man who broke out of the hospital, is that he got beat up trying to help some girl or girls. Maybe we'll never know and as I just said I will not dig unless you tell me to. Is that fair?"

"I really appreciate your help on all of this. If you could possibly get Juan, Mary, and Alice here, at, let's say 4PM, that would be great. We will be fine until then. I have a cell number I will give you and you can call me when you know what is going on."

"Sounds like a good plan to me, I will call as soon as I know anything."

Lily and Jacob got into their car as Sparky watched them from inside the paper. Jacob looked at his mom and said, "Why did you lie to that man, Mom?"

"Jacob, you know I am a big stickler on being truthful, but for some reason I needed to buy us some time on this little mystery we have uncovered. I think we have a good idea of what happened, but for some reason Bob didn't want to make this a public thing. I will make it straight with Sparky when we get this sorted out. Does that make sense and is that OK with you, Jacob? We are in this together."

"Sure it does, Mom, this whole exploration thing might be a little more interesting than I thought it was going to be. I have to admit that when you started talking about this trip, my first thoughts were not having to go to school and meeting that pretty girl in the picture you showed me. Now the added mystery of Bob's past is starting to become very fascinating. What do we do from now until four?"

"Good question. I was thinking we would drive around and check out the area a little, and then I noticed a little café like ours when we came into town. I would like to check them out and see how they do business and have a long lunch. We could get a motel, but if it goes well this afternoon I would like to get a little future down the road. What do you think?"

Sounds good to me, I like this detective stuff. By the way, I will keep my mouth shut and won't give away anything. I'll leave that up to you."

Lily laughed and they pulled away from the paper. Sparky had been watching them talk and knew he had a real story here, but he was not sure what do with it.

———

They drove around for a while; found a little museum that was pretty interesting for Lily. Jacob was not too impressed. They came across a nice little park and decided to go to the café and have that long lunch and then come back and hang out at the park until they heard from Sparky. Lily had become a student of watching people's expressions, and how they spoke to other people. Ever since Bob had shared with her how he enjoyed it, especially when he would meet someone for the first time. She was going to pay attention to the people in this little café and take mental notes to compare with how she and Lucy interacted with their Denton customers. After their long lunch and stint of people watching they headed for the park. "What did you think of that café and the people who work there, Jacob?"

"It reminded me of our diner, Mom. The food was good and everyone seemed real nice, what about you?"

"I liked it too; I wouldn't doubt that most small town cafes are that way. I guess we will get a real good chance of checking them out in the next week or so."

At about fifteen minutes past three Lily's phone rang and it was Sparky telling her that everything was set for four that afternoon. All three of them will be here. Lily thanked him and said they would be there also. Lily looked and Jacob and said, "Now we have to start the hardest part of this trip."

"What's that, Mom?"

"Telling people who might have really cared for Bob that he is gone."

Lily didn't want to get there until she was sure that everyone else was there, so she walked in with Jacob right at four. There was a different man setting at the front desk and when they came in he asked if she was Lily. When she said yes, he got up and took them to the conference room. Sparky was sitting at the head of the table and there was a couple on one side and a lady on the other. When the door opened Sparky got up and introduced everyone and said to Lily; "Call me if you need anything."

Lily thanked him and Sparky left the room, closing

the door behind him. Lily wanted to grab Jacob and run back to Denton and hide. She now knew what it was like for policemen when they had to go to someone's house and tell them that a loved one had just been killed in an accident or a senseless murder. Lily thanked them for coming. She took out the only photo of Bob she had. "I believe that Sparky told you I asked you come because we think you might be friends of Bob, and just to make sure we are talking about the same man, would you mind looking at this picture of the Bob I know and tell me if you know him. This is a picture of him and Jacob about ten years ago."

Juan and Mary looked at it and handed it Alice. Juan said, "We know this Bob very well and what is this all about?"

Lily did not answer but looked at Alice for her response. Alice said, "This is the same man who was a patient at the hospital where I work."

Lily took the picture back and then sat down at the other end of the table. Jacob had already sat down in a chair on the side of the room. "There is no easy way to do this.... She paused for a few seconds, trying to keep her composure, it didn't work, and she started sobbing and said, "Bob died last Wednesday in a fire while he was rescuing a couple of young kids."

Juan jumped up, "Oh my God, this has to be a mistake! Are you sure? No, no this can't be true!"

Mary was sobbing, she stood and Juan held her.

Alice looked at Lily and said, "Did your Bob have trauma to his eye and ear?" Lily just nodded her head yes. Alice didn't cry, but she looked very angry. Alice looked at Lily and then at Juan and Mary and said, "I have a lot of questions for all three of you, would you mind if I asked them now?"

Lily said, "The reason that Jacob and I are on this trip that will take us all the way to Montana and Oregon is for the express reason of getting some questions answered."

"Are you two OK with that?" Alice directed toward Juan and Mary. They both nodded. "If you are up to it, Lily, would you please tell us what happened?"

Lily explained the mysterious fire and how Bob got the kids out but was unable to get out himself. How Reilly got him out and what Bob said to her before he died. She then showed them the card with their names on it.

When Alice saw Kerry and Molly's name on the card she immediately said, "I got to know Bob a little when he was in the hospital, but why are my daughter and her friend's names on that card?"

Lily said, "I don't know why any of these names are on here, I was hoping you folks could help us with that."

Juan and Mary sat down and Juan said, "Give me a minute, I think I can answer most of your questions." Mary put her hand on Juan's arm; he looked at her and said, "It will be OK. First of all, let me give you a little bit of back ground on our family's relationship with Bob. I met Bob at a football game many years ago. I saw something in him and just wanted to get to know him a little bit. We had coffee that night and he ended up staying with us for a few days. Every year since then he would stop by on his way through this area. It was so cool, every year for many years he would show up about this time. Except for the last couple of years, he would always show up during one of our boy's Friday night football games. It got to be a thing with the four of us as to who would see him first. He would always go to the same spot every time. When we saw him, Mary and I would go greet him and make him sit in the stands with us. He felt a little uncomfortable with this, so we would put his back pack in our car before we brought him up into the stands. The reason he was uncomfortable was he did not want to embarrass us with him carrying a back pack and all. The boys loved him too. After the game they would run over and hug him as soon as they saw he was there. For several years Bob would take off Saturday morning with our two boys; all with back packs on and they would go up into the mountains and not come back until Sunday afternoon. The boys loved it and so did we. Mary and I made it into our special weekend alone. Think about it, Bob was camping out every night and here is going camping again with our kids. Then if we could talk him into staying another day or two, he would insist on doing a project of some kind or another around the house. I remember when Jess, our youngest, left for college, he said he was really going to miss seeing Bob and there camping trip. That does not even come close to telling you what he meant to us."

Mary said, "I remember when we could talk him into staying at least another day, he and I would see Juan off to work and the boys off to school, and Bob and I would just sit at the kitchen table talking and drinking coffee most of the morning. One time Juan asked me what we talked about and I remember reflecting on that question. I realized during those little chats it was me doing most of the talking. When Bob did talk, it was never about himself. He would say the most encouraging things about Juan and the boys, and he was always able to lift me up as a person. He was always able to somehow; make me feel better about myself. Every time he left, we would all watch him walk down the road. I knew I would miss him but then I would start looking forward to seeing him again in six months or so. He made us a better family for knowing him." Mary started to sob again.

"Well, I believe that gives you an idea of what we think of him." Juan said, "Now to address some of your other questions. Lily and Jacob, I don't know if you know that I am a probation officer. Because of this job, it puts me in a position of having to follow the letter of the law real close. When Bob called Mary and asked us to come up to see him, it put us in a bit of an awkward situation. You see Bob didn't want to have the hospital administration and the sheriff digging into his past. To this day I don't know why he was so secretive about his past, and although I am very curious, it was never a factor with us. However, I think the real reason he didn't want to hang around was that he was protecting some people. Now what I am about to tell would be best left in this room. After I tell you what I know, I hope you will feel the same way I do about leaving this alone, but that's your decision. We took Bob some clothes that night and fifteen minutes after we left, he walked out of the hospital and we gave him a ride to The Grove to pick up his pack back which he'd hidden in the bushes. He stayed at my folk's cabin for a few days and then headed off down the road like nothing ever happened. I'm sure you're wondering what happened in that grove of trees. I'm going to tell you what Bob told Mary and me. If you go to the sheriff with this it will probably cost me my job, but I think you deserve to know. Bob was going to camp in the area of that grove before he would come into our place the next day. He heard a girl screaming and ended up trying to help her and that's when he got hit in the side of the head by someone he didn't see. They worked him over pretty good and he woke up in the hospital. He gave me the names of five people. He wanted me to keep an eye on these people and possibly help them out with a little guidance if they needed it. Of the names he gave me, two were girls, and his main concern was that if at any time these girls were being threaten or hassled by the boys on the list, I was to contact him at The Denton Diner. Now with my position I have access to more information that most and I also have a friend that works for the high school which helps. I talked to this friend last Friday and found out that the three boys have not missed one day of school in the last two weeks and all three of them are playing football. It was almost a given that these three boys would not graduate from high school, now it looks like if they work hard the rest of the year, they will. Concerning the two girls; both were good students, but now they're even better. Now you can draw your own conclusions as to why Bob decided to handle this situation like he did instead of pressing attempted murder charges. For me, I staked my career on his choices and I would do it again. Not so much because of the path he chose but because of him."

When it was obvious that Juan was not only finished but struggling with his emotions, Alice let out a sigh and said, "I would like to take a turn. I don't know Lily and Jacob's relationship with Bob yet but I have a feeling it was pretty close. Obviously I didn't get to know Bob like the rest of you. I was his nurse for only two nights. That's it, two nights... and in two nights that man touched my life. In my job I see different people every day. Some of them are very nice; some are downright mean and everything in between. At first my interest in Bob was the mystery behind him. He wouldn't give up hardly any information what so ever. The first night I talked to him, I was doing what nurses are supposed to do when nursing a man who had almost been beat to death. I remember he asked me if anyone had been hurt or missing from the night before and when I told him none, to my knowledge, he seemed relieved. I looked him in his good eye and said, you got beat half to death because you were helping someone else, didn't you? He didn't say anything, but I knew that was the case. As I was leaving the room I turned to him and said, would you do it over again, and he just gave me a little nod. He also had a wonderful, dry sense of humor. It's funny, the first time I came into his room, when he was awake that first night; he was almost out of his bed. I said, 'What do you think you are doing?' Do you know what is reply was? He said something like he was going out to dinner and a movie and if I paid my own way, I could go. Then I almost had to wrestle him to get him to use a bed pan."

Everyone laughed and then Alice said, "When I walked into his room the night he left, I couldn't find him and then I saw a note on his pillow. It was a warm, sappy note telling me encouraging things. I sat on the edge of his bed and wept. I have never done that before in 19 years of nursing. Now after listening to what Juan said it looks like I owe that man more that a fond memory. Well, that is enough out of me; I would really like to hear from Lily and Jacob."

Lily looked at Jacob and said, "I just loved listening to all of you talk about Bob and how he affected your lives. It has prompted me to share some things that I have not shared with anyone, not even Jacob. We are very lucky in that Bob was in Denton for several months every year for the last fifteen." She told them about how they met, about Reilly and the travel trailer. Things he did for others, about the time the put a new roof on the diner, about Reilly and Lucy getting married again and how he made her spend more time at home with Jacob. Then she said, "Unlike all of you, I didn't treat Bob the way he deserved."

She dabbed her eyes and continued, "I treated Bob

like a good friend, a trustworthy employee, and a great father figure to my son." She paused, "I also treated him like a transient." She told them about the night before the fire, everything, Luke and Larry, those two wonderful dances and even the kiss. "I realized that night that I had been holding every guy who wanted to date me to Bob's standards, and none of them came close. I also realized that I loved him with all of my heart." Then she told them about the conversation with Annie York and what she'd had learned about Pat and Sammy and that Pat had gotten married and Bob was so glad for her and that maybe it was time for him to settle down. "I think he was going to possibly settle down in Denton with Jacob and me. It might not be right, to sum that all up in a couple of dances and a kiss, but I really feel he had plans to stay in Denton, and I blew it. If I would have taken my mind off of him being a transient a long time ago, things would have been different."

There was a silence and then Jacob who had been silent said, "Mom, if that would have happened, these people would never have known him for who he was and I know that there are some folks down the road who wouldn't have known him either."

"Thank you Jacob, you're absolutely correct, however, I know I will be a long time forgiving myself for having a mindset that pigeon holes people for whatever reason."

They exchanged phone numbers and addresses and promised to stay in touch. Mary gave Lily and Jacob each a big hug and then she and Juan left. "I really want to know more about what you find out about Bob's life," Alice said. "I would also like to come to Denton to visit you and bring my daughter and her friend."

"I would like that Alice," replied Lily. Alice hugged

each of them and left.

Lily and Jacob were standing when Sparky came into the conference room. "Did everything go OK?" Sparky asked.

"It did, not easy, but OK."

"I am glad, is there anything else I can help you with?"

"Sparky you have been most gracious for helping us. You have made this whole process a lot easier for all of us and we appreciate it. We all know a lot more now than we did this morning and I know that you probably see the potential for an interesting story in all of this. I guess what I am trying to say Sparky, is that I would appreciate it if you would let this story pass by for now. Is that fair?"

"Of course it is Lily, what are to going to do now?"

"We are headed for Lone Tree, Montana, with a few stops along the way. Our goal is to find some people who we think were close to Bob, and to maybe fill in some of the gaps in Bob's past that we know nothing about."

"It sounds like you are going have an interesting time; I would sure like to know about your results when you get finished with your journey."

"That's a request that I think we will hear often in the next week or so and we plan to document as much we can. Please give me your card and we will let you know what we find out. Jacob, let's head for Rock River, Utah!"

When Alice got home, Kerry and Molly were in the living room watching TV. "Hey girls, how was school today?" Alice said as she stood looking at them.

"It was OK," Kerry said, "Where have you been?"

Alice looked at Kerry for a few seconds and then said, "Could we turn the TV off?"

Kerry clicked the off button on the remote control and said, "What's up, Mom?"

Alice sat down in a chair across from the girls. "Myself, and a couple from here in Elmira, got a call requesting we meet this woman and her son from Denton. She was here because she had a friend who had died in an accident last week. The reason she called us was that this friend had our names on a card that he had in his Bible. Her friend was the man who was in the hospital that you girls met that time you came up to see me. Do you remember him?"

The girls looked at each other and then Molly, with a slight quiver in her voice said, "His name was Bob... wasn't it?"

"Yes it was."

Kerry, obviously disturbed by the news of Bob's death said, "How did he die, Mom?"

"Apparently there was a fire and Bob ended up saving two little kids that were trapped in that fire, but he didn't make it," Alice said with an obvious tremor in her voice.

Kerry looked at Molly, and with tears coming down her face said, "I have to tell her, Molly, I have to tell my mom everything!"

CHAPTER 20

It was almost nine that night when Lily and Jacob pulled into Rock River, Utah. They found one of only two motels in the little town and checked in. As they were leaving the motel office, Lily turned and asked the lady who checked them in, "Would you happen to know of anyone in town by the name of Lat or Kate?"

The lady laughed and said, "There are a grand total of 325 people in this thriving little town. We have a Kate or two, but we only have one Lat and his wife's name is Kate. Why do you ask?"

Lily found herself being somewhat reserved about offering too much information on their true agenda. She looked at the lady and decided she would do most of the asking. The first thing that came to her mind was Bob's knack for sizing people up when he first met them. This woman, who looked like she was around 110 years old but probably closer to 70, should have intrigued her right away. But because Lily just wanted the comfort of a decent room with a hot shower, she did not see the fact that this was probably a very interesting person. It was late in the evening in a sleepy little town and the lady who checked them in was smoking a cigarette and drinking a bottle of beer right in front of Lily and her son. This should have been a clue to something.

Who is this lady and what was her life's story? What did she know about Lat and Kate, and maybe even Bob? "Do you know them?" Lily said and before the lady could reply, Lily said, "I'm sorry, my name is Lily and this is my son Jacob," and she put her hand out to the woman.

The woman shook Lily's hand as well as Jacob's and

said, "My name is Crit and I am very glad to meet both of you. My dad use to call me critter because I was always collecting animals, then they just started calling me Crit. My real name is Tabatha; what kind of name is that? Do I look like a Tabatha to you Jacob?"

"Well I guess not," said Jacob, "But I like Crit."

As she was putting out her cigarette and taking a drink of her beer she said, "Do I know a Lat and Kate? Yes, I do, as matter of fact, know them very well." She took another drink of beer and lit a cigarette and said, "It's your turn, why do you want to know?"

Lily thought of the hot shower for a second then realized that this woman was probably crazier than a June bug, but was probably also the real deal. She also thought about the fact that if Bob spent any time in a town of this size he probably knew a lot of the locals, just like any other place that he spent time. Lily took out the picture of Bob and showed it to her and said, "Crit, do you recognize this man?"

She took a drag on her cigarette and said, "That's Bob! What are you doing with a picture of my Bob?" She said it with a sense of fear and anxiety. Crit sat down in a chair behind the counter and said again, "Why do you have his picture?"

Lily could see in her face a look of... please do not give me any bad news about this man. Lily's emotions started to boil up in her as soon as seen the expression on this little woman's face. All Lily could think of was being as straight forward with her as she could be. Then she remembered that in one of the pieces of paper in Bob's Bible was a drawing of a fawn with a beautiful little smile, and above that that drawing was the word, Crit. Oh my, she said to herself, this is not getting any easier. "Crit, Bob died in accident last week."

It was just like all the air went out of an inflated doll. Crit sat back in her chair with her head down as if the life had been pulled from her. Then as quickly as the life went out of her, she jumped back up. "What happened," she demanded, "What happen? Who are you and what happened to him? Don't sissy around, what happened to him?" She sobbed and looked Lily in face and said, "What happened to my Angel?"

By this time Jacob was standing beside his mom holding her, looking at this woman who was another of the many people that this man had crossed paths with in his transient life. The time for being reserved and withholding information was behind them. Lily looked at Crit and said with all of the self composure she could muster, "There was a fire and Bob died saving two little kids." She left it hanging out there like grass in the wind.

Finally, Crit said; "I knew it, I knew that little bugger would do something like this. I knew he was destined to do something like this. I knew he wouldn't come back here and rescue me from this place. You two go get settled in to your room and I'll be over in about fifteen minutes. I don't care how tired you are, I have some questions and the room is on me."

Lily was just getting out of the shower when she heard a knock on their door. Jacob opened the door and without any pretense, Crit walked in with a bag filled with sandwiches in one hand and a six pack of beer in the other. She put several quarters in Jacob's hand and said, "There is a pop machine down the hall, get what you want." Crit put a chair by the opened door and opened a beer and lit a cigarette and said, "Don't hold back and I won't."

Lily felt like she was is in the presence of someone she'd known for years. She felt rejuvenated. "Are those cold?"

"Cold as they're going to get."

"I guess that is cold enough."

Crit opened a bottle and handed it to Lily, and said, "What happened?"

Crit didn't interrupt as Lily told her about the fire, the past fifteen years, and the hardest part, the details of the night before Bob died and how she finally realized how she really felt about him. Crit opened another beer after she dabbed her eyes with a tissue, and said, "I guess you are one of dumbest bimbos I have ever met. My dear Lord girl, how could you be around a man like that and not understand who he really was? Oh well, what happens now? Are we going to carry on with this whinny stuff, or are we going to get on with it? What do you think that ol' rambler would have us do? Do you think he would want us to be all sad and sappy, or go on with our lives? I don't know, but I think I'll go get really drunk. Before I do that though...Lat and Kate..."

Laturaus Felt was a typical, young, on fire for Jesus preacher out of the Bible belt of America. He was raised with the whole concept of church and family. When he first received the invitation to apply for the position of senior pastor of Rock River Christian Fellowship in Rock River, Utah his first thoughts were jubilant. An invitation for a senior pastor position right out of seminary was really exciting. His first interview was somewhat discouraging. We are in a world of Mormon influence he was informed. We are here to hold a position and to do the best we can. After a very short second interview comprised of a few questions and answers he was offered the position of senior pastor of River Rock Christian Fellowship. His salary, as humble it may be, was the best they could do. They would try to find him and or his wife work. Why did he feel like he was part of a long list of pastors who had tried and failed in this Fellowship? With all the pomp and vigor that a young couple fresh out of seminary could muster, Lat and Kate embraced the invitation and became members of the small community of Rock River. They would do their best to spread the gospel of Jesus Christ.

"Here's the deal," Crit said with a sigh, "I lost my husband to a heart attack about twelve years ago. He had his faults, just like all of us. He thought he was a lady's man the way he flirted with just about every woman who stayed in this here motel of ours. I never gave him a bad time about it. I know he never messed around on me; he just liked the girls, I guess. He loved this little town and just about everyone in it. He was everything to me and not long after he died I started drinking to pretend to cover up the pain. It doesn't work, but I still do it. About five years after Bill died, Lat and Kate moved into town. They were young and all full of Jesus and saving the world by starting with us poor lost souls in Rock River. The bunch that runs that little church they are at went through pastors on a regular basis. It got so I didn't know who was coming or going. These pastors would come by once in a while to try and get us to come to church. We were always busy with the motel so never did go."

After lighting another cigarette, Crit continued, "The first time Lat stopped in I was not having a very good day and didn't treat him real sociable like. I kind of told him that if he was going to come around preaching at me, he just as well not come around. I think I kind of scared him, because he didn't come by for a long time. I would see him at the grocery store once in awhile and we would say hello, but that was about it. One day Kate came in to see me. I had met her a few times and thought she was a pretty sweet little thing. Her parents were coming to visit and they didn't have room for them in their little house, so she was checking on the cost of a room. I remember it like it was yesterday. After I told her what my rates were she got this kind of sad look on her face and said thanks and was heading for the door. I said, "Wait a minute, Kate, what's the matter?"

She looked at me and with a hesitation in her voice, "We just can't afford it and my parents have just enough money to get here and back to their home in Idaho. The church can't afford to pay us much. Lat is working part time for a local rancher, but it doesn't pay very well either. I don't know what to do," Kate said with tears welling up in her eyes.

"We ended up making a deal that she would help me with cleaning when I had a busy night," Crit said. "We've worked together every since. The reason I'm telling you this is that little gal is pretty special to me. I like Lat a lot, but Kate is like a daughter to me."

It was time for another cigarette and beer and then Crit said, "I forgot about these sandwiches, you two help yourselves, you must be hungry."

Lily and Jacob were hungry and the tuna fish sandwiches were perfect.

Crit paused and with obvious emotion he her voice said, "Bob is a major reason why I've gotten so close to those kids. Five or six years ago I saw Bob around their church. In fact if you go out in the parking lot you can see the church right down the street. Anyway he was there for a few days and then I didn't see him again for about six months. I can see half of the town from my office window and being the snoop that I am, I saw Bob at the church messing around the flower beds. We all tell each other that we are watching out for each other, which is true, but we really are a bunch of snoops. In this town if a cat crosses the street it is news, so when a stranger is hanging around we all put our snoop hats on. I decided I would walk over and see if we had a new member of our little town. As I was crossing the street, Lat came walking out of the church. Lat greeted me and then introduced me to Bob. I was taken right away by his humble, gentle manor, but what really impressed me was the kindness in his eyes. I am telling you, Lily and Jacob, after talking to him for only a few minutes, I was ready to bundle him up and take him home. Anyway we were making small talk when Kate came out of the church. After a few more minutes of small talk, Kate invited me to have supper with them that evening. You can see the parking lot of the motel from the little house they have next to the church, so I wasn't worried about leaving for an hour or so. We had a wonderfully pleasant evening. It was so calm and relaxing, that I didn't realize I hadn't had a cigarette. For me to go that long without a smoke is very unusual. Before I left I asked Bob where he was staying. Almost apologetically, he told me that Lat and Kate were letting him sleep in the church. I looked at him and said I have a few things that can use fixing, if you want to mess around repairing some stuff, you are welcome to a room at the motel in trade, if you would like. He looked at Lat, I think for his approval. Lat told him that would be real nice for both him and me and that was that. He stayed in room 115 every time he came to town."

Crit lit another cigarette and seemed to be in deep

thought.

Lily finished the last bite of her sandwich and said, "This is not easy for you is it?"

"No... it isn't. It shouldn't be a big deal. I mean the man was only here for about week in the spring and a week in the fall. He was here and before you knew it he was gone. I don't know, it's not like he performed miracles or anything when he was here. I guess I just felt such a peace within myself when he was around. He would putt around here and at the church. He would just do stuff. He was so unassuming and always so appreciative of the littlest things. Whenever we talked he'd listen and I would just rattle on. No one ever made me feel so comfortable just saying what was on my mind. He knew how to make you feel good about yourself. Do you know what I mean?"

"I sure do," Lily said. "I guess I realized it the most when I started looking out the window of our diner all the time when it was getting close to the time of year he would come back to Denton. Every spring when I knew he would be leaving soon I would start fretting about the fact that he was leaving. I would tell myself it was all in my head. I convinced myself I was going to miss him because he would not be around to open and close the diner or fix things for me. I realize now that I would miss him for much more than that. He was a wonderful friend and...I know now... that I truly loved him."

Lily was quietly sobbing when Jacob sat down beside her, and put his arm around her and said, "We met some people in Elmira yesterday who knew Bob well. This couple told us about how he would take their boys camping and how much the boys enjoyed it. He would take me camping, too. The first time mom let us stay out in the desert overnight, I was only seven years old. The last time was just last year, when I was sixteen. Whenever I told my friends we had been camping, some would be jealous and some would say how boring it must be to sleep out in the dirt with no TV or video games. It was never boring. I realize now how much I enjoyed and looked forward to those camping trips. He taught me so much about surviving in the outdoors, but he also taught me about myself. We would talk about my future, not so much about a career, but what kind of person I wanted to be. I remember he always made a big deal of how I treated others, especially my mom. He would tell me Bible stories that I had heard before, but when he told them, they seemed to come to life and make so much more sense. I remember he would create survival games, where he would give me clues and some directions and then he would tell me he would meet me at a certain place in the desert. As I got older the challenges would get harder. The cool thing was...I was never scared. One time I did mess up and got myself completely lost. It was late in the day and I knew it was going to get dark pretty soon. I sat down on a rock and remembered what Bob had taught me. I gathered some firewood and then made myself a shelter. Not long after I started a fire, Bob walked into my camp and asked me if I would share it with him. He had been watching me the whole time. It was always like that. Bob was always there for me when I needed him, even when he was gone. I know one thing, if I ever have kids; I'll do my best to treat them like Bob treated me."

"How come I never heard about you being lost in the desert?" Lily said.

"We were afraid if we told you, you wouldn't let me go anymore."

They all laughed and Crit said, "How are we going to deal with telling Lat and Kate? It's getting kind of late, but

I can get them over here right now or we can tell them in the morning."

"If you don't mind I'd rather wait until tomorrow." Lily replied.

"I'm sure that will be fine. You two get a good night's sleep and when you're ready I'll take you over to their place or we can have them come over here. Is that OK?"

"That will be fine and thank you for everything."

When Lily and Jacob walked into the motel office the next morning Crit had coffee made and some pastries on a plate. "Good morning you two, I hope you got some sleep."

"We did OK," Lily said, "How about you?"

"I've had much better nights, to tell you the truth. Shall I call Lat and Kate and see if they want to come over?"

"I tell you Crit, this whole process of telling people about Bob doesn't get any easier. But I know it has to be done and we are looking forward to meeting them."

"OK, I'll call them and invite them over for coffee."

Lat and Kate were able to come right over and after all of the introductions, everyone sat down in Crit's living room. The atmosphere of the room was very uncomfortable for everyone and Crit broke the ice by saying, "The reason I called you over to meet Lily and Jacob is they are friends of Bob and they have something they want to tell us."

Lily was looking at the floor twisting a paper napkin she had in her hand. She looked up, took a deep breath and said, "I am sorry to tell you that last Wednesday Bob died in an accident. There was a fire in an abandoned building and Bob died saving the lives of two children that were trapped inside."

"Crit, do you know about this? Are we sure it's our Bob?" Lat said in a demanding tone.

"Yes, Lily and Jacob got here last night. They showed me a picture and it's our Bob. It was late so we decided to wait until this morning to tell you two. I hope we didn't offend you by waiting to tell you this morning."

"That's not a problem at all. I just can't believe that he's gone. He died saving some kids, that's amazing, but so sad. Isn't that so typical of Bob though? I know that Bob was the type of guy to not hesitate to lay his life on the line for someone else. I'm so glad that he had such a wonderful relationship with God. I know where he is right now and as sad as I am for his death, his new life with Jesus is real and I am happy for him in that respect."

Kate, with tears running down her face said, "These are the two who Bob talked about so much. He would never talk about himself, but he would talk about you two a lot. Could you tell us more about what happened and about your relationship with Bob? Is that too personal?"

It seemed to Lily that she had told this story so many times before, with great difficulty, but this time it felt different. She didn't struggle as much, and she felt a sense of pride in telling about Bob and his relationship with herself and Jacob and everyone else in Denton. That was the case until she got to part about the night before he died. With more tears she told them about how much she loved him." She paused and said, "Last night Crit told me I must be the dumbest bimbo she ever met for not realizing what a wonderful person Bob was, and she is right. Jacob and I are trying to do right by him by finding as many people as we can who knew him."

Lat obviously struggling with his emotions said, "I am not surprised that Crit called you a bimbo. Not because you may be one but because she has called me that on numerous occasions." They all laughed and Lat went on to say, "I need to ask each of you a very personal but important question. After knowing who Bob was and what he stood for as a man, what is your relationship with Jesus Christ?"

"Do you think this is the right time to do some preaching Lat?" Crit said a bit indignantly.

"All I know Crit, is I loved that man and I know he loved Jesus and I also know he loved Lily and Jacob. You know who else he really loved, Crit? You! He thought the world of all three of you. I also know that Bob was the type of guy who showed his Christianity by his actions and not with words. I wouldn't be able to sleep at night if I didn't ask this question before Lily and Jacob left. I'm sorry I just need to know."

"Please don't be sorry, Lat," Lily said. "If you think of anything that would be important to Bob, I want to know about it. In my case it's good that you asked, because Bob never did. I kept expecting him to. I knew he was a Christian, not only because of the way he treated others, but by the amount of time he put into reading the Bible, and I assume, praying. He would sit on the porch of that old shack that burned down, or go off into the desert for hours, with that old Bible in his hand. I have always thought of myself as a Christian, but mainly because I figured I was a pretty decent person and the other religions didn't make much sense to me. I do know something for sure, I don't have the type of relationship with Jesus Christ that Bob had. Maybe I should be asked that question of yours. Maybe it is about time I quit avoiding it. Do you know what I mean?"

"I know very well what you mean Lily, but before I answer I would love to hear from Jacob or Crit."

Crit, obviously disturbed by the way the conversation had changed, got up and went to the door, opened it and lit a cigarette. She was just about to say something when Jacob, in low voice said, "Last spring before Bob left for Montana we went on one of our many camping trips. It was our first day out and we had gone several miles. We were both tired and decided to set up camp. After we had had a bite to eat we were sitting by a little camp fire watching the sun go down, Bob reached into his back pack and took out his Bible and started reading it. This wasn't unusual as he did this often. In the past he would sometimes tell me stories from the Bible but he never asked me to read it or what I thought of his stories or the Bible or even God. This particular time I asked him why he never questioned me on what I thought of all this Bible stuff. I remember it so well. He paused a few seconds and then said, 'I was waiting for the right time. I was waiting for the time when you as a person were ready to hear what I have to say about what it really means to be a Christian.'"

"Then he told me that God is very real. That Jesus Christ really did die on the cross so that we would not only have our sins forgiven but have eternal life. This didn't really click for me until he explained the simple fact that if we ask Jesus to come into our heart and confess Him as our Lord and Savior he would give us the best thing we could ever have. Then he told me that a lot of people say that prayer but really don't mean it or believe it. They say it because someone asked them too or someone they like or respected did it. After that, they would say they know who Christ is and that they are saved and might even go to church and hang out with other church goers, but most of the time their lives didn't change that much. They would act one way around their church friends and a different way with others. The point he made so clear to me was that in order to be truly a Christian you had say that prayer and really mean it. Then you had to repent and turn your life over to God. If a person would really turn their life over to God they would learn who He really is. Then he asked me what I thought about all of that. I told him I needed to think about it. 'He said OK and that if I ever had any questions he would do his best to answer them.' Before he left for Montana he gave me a Bible that he said he had bought for me several years ago. To answer your question Lat, I started reading that Bible and praying and the night before Bob died he led me to the Lord and I know that it is real and the more mom and I follow Bob's footsteps the realer it gets."

Lily, who was obviously spell-bound by what Jacob was saying, said, "Jacob, honey, how come you never told me anything about this?"

"Well, Mom, one of the things I learned from Bob was to be patient. I knew there would be a right time and I was just waiting for it. I didn't think that that time would be in front of so many people, but that's OK. I am extremely excited on where this whole Christian thing is going."

Kate with a big smile on her face said, "Jacob that was beautiful and you will never know how excited I am for you. Thank you for sharing that so honestly."

Crit had finished her smoke but was still standing at the door looking out. There was a short silence and then she said, "I know you are all waiting on me, right? Well, I'm not all that sure I want to spill my guts out to all of you about how I feel about God and all that stuff. I will tell you one thing...because of Bob I have thought about it a lot. I also have thought a lot about it because of Kate, and even you Lat. I know that with my age and drinking and smoking the way I do I don't have a lot of time left. Give me a little time to sort through all of this."

Kate was watching Crit intensely and with obvious love in her eyes. Lat was looking at her the same way and he said, "You know, Crit, that Kate and I love you very much and for you to say those words puts joy in my heart. You take as much time as you want, but it is very important that you start praying to God to give you the answers you need to make that decision. I think you already know that Kate and I will be here for you if need anything, anything at all."

"Thanks Lat, I have known for a long time that I could count on you two."

Lat looked at Lily and said, "Lily I would like nothing better than to lead you to salvation in Christ right here and now, but I think that on this journey you and Jacob are taking, there will be a time when you will lay your life before the Lord. When that time comes your own son will lead you. That's very exciting to me."

"I'm pretty excited myself and I think Bob would like that as well." Lily replied.

Kate with more tears in her eyes said, "More than we will ever know, Lily."

Crit finally returned to her seat and said, "Can I change the subject without offending anyone?" Before anyone could answer she said, "Was there any kind of memorial fund set up in Bob's name? You know what I mean; usually it's to a cancer or heart fund of some kind."

Lily with a concerned look on her face said, "Well,

no Crit, there wasn't. We never thought of it, but it sure is a good idea. Does anyone have anything in mind?"

"You told us about Bob's attorney friend. Did he leave any kind of instructions with her?" Kate asked.

"The only thing was Bob had some money in the bank in Denton and we were told he wanted us to use whatever we needed to make this trip, and he wanted the rest used to help Jacob and the Sammy girl I told you about in Montana with their college expenses."

Crit smiled and said, "There you go, you can set up a college fund in his name. I bet a lot of people who would give to that if they knew about it."

"I think that's a great idea Crit. What better way to help remember Bob than a fund that helps kids. What do you think Lily?" asked Kate.

"I like it too. I could write the folks I have already seen and I think the newspaper man in Elmira will even put it in the paper for us. We'll do it. I'll talk to Sammy's mom about it and we'll put something together. I'll call the bank in Denton before we leave and establish an account in his name."

Lat said, "This has been a very interesting morning, to say the least. What are you going to do next?"

Lily looked at Jacob and said, "I think we are headed for Bolt, Colorado."

"Really?" said Lat, "That's a little cow town about 200 miles east of here. I have been there, it's a beautiful place."

CHAPTER 21

The drive from Rock River to Bolt was breathtaking. Traveling through the Rocky Mountains any time of year was wonderful but in the fall, with all of the different, rich, autumn colors made it truly special for Lily and Jacob. They pulled into Bolt to find a very small town with no stoplights and only a few stores. Lily parked and said, "What do think Jacob, I saw a little motel, do you want to get a room, or try to find Jack and Jess first?"

"There's a sheriff's office right across the street, why don't we see if anyone in there knows them and go from there. I'm kind of anxious to see what this next chapter in Bob's life is all about."

"Me too, let's go find out."

They walked into the office to find a middle aged officer setting behind a desk reading a newspaper. He was quite large and had a chewed up cigar in his mouth. He put the paper down he was reading and said, "What can I do for you folks?"

"We're looking for some people who we think might live here and were wondering if you might help us?" Lily said.

"I guess that depends on who they are and why you're looking for em."

"We don't have any last names, but what we do have is Jack and Jess and a Jimmy."

"Doesn't sound like you know these folks very well, now does it?"

Lily sensing the doubt in his tone said, I'm sorry, my name is Lily Fields, and this is my son Jacob. We're from

Denton, Arizona. A friend of ours died recently and in his belongings was this card."

She handed him the card, which he studied for a minute and said, "What was your friend's name?"

"Bob, Bob Dolan. Here's a picture of him, maybe you recognize him?"

"I'm the sheriff of this county; my name is Bud March. I know Bob, he's been coming through here for several years. First time I met him, I liked him. He was a real good man and I'm sorry to hear he died. How did it happen?"

"There was a fire and he died saving a little boy and girl."

"My, that's really too bad. I know all three of these people. Jack and Jessica Nisbet have a spread about ten miles north of here. They are good people. I know Bob would stay with them whenever he passed through. Jimmy lives right here in town. Jimmy is mentally retarded and I have a feeling he is going to take this pretty hard. If you want to see these folks, I suggest you go talk to Jack and Jessica first and maybe they can help you with Jimmy. I can give Jack and Jess a call and see if they're home."

"You're being very kind. Please call them and ask if them if it would be possible for us to drive out this afternoon."

On the third ring Jessica Nisbet answered, "Hello."

"Jessica, this is Bud March."

"Hi Bud, how are you today?"

"Oh, I am fine Jessica. I have a couple people here who would like to come out and visit you and Jack this afternoon; would that be OK with you?"

"Who are they Bud? Do we know them, they're not salesman are they?"

"No, they're not salesman, Jessica, they're good people and they would just like to talk to the two of you."

"Well Bud, if you say so, send them on out. Jack is right outside, we'll both be here."

"They will be out in a little bit, good bye Jessica."

When they pulled up to the ranch house 20 minutes later Jessica Nisbet came out wiping her hands on her apron. Lily could see the kindness in this woman's face before she even got out of her car. Lily and Jacob got out and walked up to her and Lily extended her hand and said, "Mrs. Nisbet my name is Lily Fields and this is my son Jacob. Thank you so much for letting us come here to see you and Mr. Nisbet."

As they were shaking hands, Jack came out of the house and Jessica said, "I'm pleased to meet you, Lily and Jacob, please call me Jess. This is my husband Jack."

Jack stepped down and shook both their hands and said, "Nice to meet you folks, won't you come in and we'll see what we can do for you?"

They all went into the kitchen and Jess offered them a seat at the large kitchen table and something to drink. Both Lily and Jacob declined and Lily said, "I will get right to the point. We are friends of Bob Dolan and after talking to the sheriff we know that you are as well. But just to be sure, I would like you to look at a picture of our Bob."

Jess took the picture, and after looking at it handed it to Jack who said, "This is the Bob we know, however, we never knew his last name. What is this all about?"

Lily looked him right in the eyes and said, "I am very sorry to have to tell you this... last Wednesday there was a fire and Bob died saving the lives of two little kids."

Jack stood up and with a very stern voice said, "This better not be some kind of joke."

Lily, now looking down into her lap said, "I am afraid it's very true."

Jack stood there for a second and then tears started to well up in his eyes, "Please excuse me," he grabbed his hat and walked out the door.

"We're so sorry to bring this news to you Jess, but we just felt we had to."

"Oh, I completely understand Lily and it's very kind of you to come all this way to tell us. You live in Denton, Arizona don't you?"

"Why, yes we do, how did you know?"

"We've known Bob for several years and he didn't tell us much about himself, but he did talk about you two often. It was obvious that he thought a great deal of both of you. Jack and I were happy that he spent his winters down there. I thought the world of Bob, but I didn't realize until this moment how much he meant to my Jack. We have received word of friends and family members passing on in the past, but I've never seen him react like this before. When Bob would stop and stay with us for a few days, Jack and him were always out doing something together. At first, we would tell him he didn't have to help around here when he visited. He would just say he enjoyed working with Jack and couldn't think of just laying around doing nothing. When Jack tried paying him he would politely let us know that that was never an option and he said my cooking was more than enough pay for what he did. I don't know that my cooking was all that good, but Bob never missed an opportunity to complement me on it and everything else around here. He really liked it here and we liked him being here."

Jack came in the back door and hung up his hat. He looked at Lily and then Jacob and politely said, "I am sorry for leaving like that. Would you please tell us what happened to Bob and we would love to know more about you two and Bob's time with you. You're the folks from Denton, Arizona aren't you?"

Lily accepted a cup of coffee and for the next hour told the Nisbets everything. When she got to the part of the night before he died, and how she realized how much she truly loved him, she broke down and cried and so did Jess for the first time.

Jess wiped the tears from her eyes and said, "You know Bob never got to meet our two boys, but every time he would come to visit he would ask about them. He wanted to know how their families were doing, and everything about them. He would always ask if we had any new pictures of our grand kids. He was genuinely interested. I could see in his eyes how much he wanted a family of his own. We knew all about you two, and Pat and Sammy in Montana, and what he thought of you. I knew though, that he dreamed of more, and I know it was with you two. He was so happy for Pat and her new husband and I think you are right, I think he was ready to settle down in Denton. However, I was afraid it would never happen because I was pretty sure he would never ask you to marry him."

"Why do you think that?" Lily asked.

"Well, it's not like we talked about it or anything. It

was just bits and pieces I picked up over the years. I don't think Bob thought he was good enough for you. In his mind I think he expected to show up one fall day and find that you had fallen love with someone and he would move on. I'm quite sure that would have broken his heart. You would never have known that though. He would have made sure you were happy and faded out of your lives. That was just the way he was. I think Bob had a tremendous amount of sorrow in his past and never would let anyone close enough to share that pain. Maybe he did with you two, but I have a feeling he never did with you either."

Lily was sobbing and said, "No... no he never would. Every time I tried he would put me off and say maybe someday."

Jess stood up and said, "Jacob you have to be one of the politest young men I have ever met. You've been sitting here for over an hour and not said one word. I bet you and your mom are both very hungry. I put a roast in before you came, it would be wonderful if you would have supper with us. What do you think?"

Lily looked at Jacob and he nodded yes and she said, "We would like that very much."

They had wonderful meal together, talking about Bob and the things he and Jack did together. They talked about studying the Bible together and how the Nisbets had been Christians since they were teenagers. They were happy to hear how things went in Rock River with Crit, Lat, and Kate. They had coffee and homemade apple pie, and were just about through eating when Lily said, "Do either of you know anything about someone named

Jimmy, and a Sally?"

Jess looked at Jack and said, "Oh my, I didn't think about Jimmy, he thought the world of Bob."

They spent the next thirty minutes of both Jess and Jack telling about Jimmy and how Bob affected his life. They told about Jimmy's house and how well he was doing and how much Sally and a half dozen other people in the community looked after him. "I've got an idea," Jack said as he was standing up. "Why don't you two stay here tonight and get a good night's sleep and we'll go see Jimmy tomorrow. I'm pretty sure he doesn't work tomorrow. What do you think Jess, would that be all right?"

"That's a wonderful idea. Would you stay, we have lots of room?"

"I don't know," Lily said, "That would be quite a burden on you two."

Jess laughed and said, "Don't be silly, it would be no trouble at all. Besides it would be very nice to get to know both of you better. Come on I'll show you your rooms."

Jack knocked on Jimmy's door the next morning and Jimmy opened it right away. With a look of surprise on his face he said, "Mr. and Mrs. Nisbet, what are you doing here? I mean welcome, or am I in trouble for something? Who are these people?"

"Hi Jimmy, this is Lily and Jacob Fields. They live down in Denton, Arizona and we just wanted to talk to you for a minute, and no, you're not in trouble."

"OK then, why don't you all come in. Do you want me to make some coffee or something?"

"Oh, no Jimmy, we don't need anything."

"I'm sorry, I don't have enough chairs for everyone. I'll have to buy me some more chairs won't I Mrs. Nisbet? What do you think of my house Mrs. Nisbet? Pretty clean isn't it? Here look at my sink...no dirty dishes, and come here and look at my bathroom, clean as a whistle isn't it?"

"Yes, Jimmy, it looks very nice. I'm so proud of you for taking such good care of your home."

"Thank you Mrs. Nisbet. What do you want to talk to me about with these people?"

Jack took a deep breath and said, "Jimmy, Lily and Jacob are friends of Bob."

"Really, where is he, is he with you?"

"Jimmy, there has been an accident, well a fire actually. Anyway, there was a fire down in Denton and two little kids where trapped in this old house, and well, Jimmy...Bob went into that old house and saved those kids. He really did, but Jimmy...Bob didn't make it. Bob died saving those kids. I'm so sorry; I know you and Bob were good friends."

Jimmy's broad grin faded away from his face and was replaced by an expression that affected all four of them. Jimmy walked over to Jess and put his arms around her and said, "Mrs. Nisbet, please tell me he's lying to me. Tell me it ain't true."

Jess held him tight and said, "I am so sorry Jimmy, Bob is gone, he is home with his Jesus now."

"He's with Jesus right now? Are sure he's with Jesus? That is good, Bob told me all about Jesus and he helped me get Jesus in my heart. He also said that someday we would be together with Jesus. I guess he's just gone on ahead and I will meet him there someday. Is that right Mrs. Nisbet?"

"That's right Jimmy. He will be waiting for all of us there."

Jimmy wiped his eyes and looked at Jacob and said, "You're the guy Bob told me about. You and Bob would go camping together, is that right?"

With a surprised look on his face, Jacob said, "Yes sir, Bob took me camping a lot."

Jacob who was obviously struggling with his emotions turned away and Jimmy said, "It's OK Jacob, I know you are going to miss him to. But he is heaven now, he's OK. Don't you worry about our friend Bob, he is with Jesus now. The reason I know about you is because Bob took me camping too. We would walk up into those hills yonder and he would teach me all kinds of stuff. He taught me how to take care of myself if I ever got stuck out there for some reason. Did he teach you that stuff too Jacob and did he read Bible stories to you like he did me?"

"Yes sir, he did."

"I don't think anyone has ever called me sir. Now I know why Bob liked you so much, you're a nice person. You sure are.

Maybe someday you and I could be friends Jacob."

"I would like that, Jimmy."

Lily said, "Jimmy we've brought you something of Bob's that I think he would like you to have."

She handed Jimmy a framed picture of a cowboy on a horse. Jimmy looked at it and said, "That is one of the neatest pictures I have ever seen. What does it say done here at the bottom."

"Well, Jimmy, this is a quote from a man named

Robert Louis Stevenson and it says, "*We are all travelers in the wilderness of this world, and the best we find in our travels is an honest friend.*" That's why Jacob and I want to give it to you. I know Bob must have thought of you as a special friend."

"Thank you very much ma'am, I have a perfect place to hang it."

"Jimmy, I also have a picture that Bob had in his Bible of you and another man."

Jimmy took the picture and said, "That is me and my brother." Jimmy sat down in the only chair he had at his little kitchen table and with his head down and said, "That is me and my brother. I loved my brother; he was real good to me, just like Bob was."

It was obvious that Jimmy was struggling when Jack said, "Jimmy, Lily and Jacob are heading north to meet some more of Bob's friends. Would you do Jess and I favor?"

"What's that Mr. Nisbet?"

"Would you come out to the ranch and help me with some cows and have lunch with us? I would sure appreciate it."

Jimmy stood up with a smile on his face and said, "I would love to Mr. Nisbet, I would like that a lot."

CHAPTER 22

Lily and Jacob had traveled over 200 miles since they left Jimmy's house. They had lunch in a wonderful little café in a small town much like Denton. The people were very nice and the food was good, maybe not as good as Lily's, but good. The drive itself was glorious. They had gone through open country where then saw deer and antelope and now they were in the mountains. They were in awe of the huge, majestic pine and fir trees, rushing rivers and beautiful lakes. Living in the desert of Arizona was so much different than this country and they both were enjoying every mile they drove. About three in the afternoon they came to a small town. Lily especially loved these small towns and they would drive around in just about everyone they came to. They enjoyed the process of getting a little bit of a feel for these towns and what kind of communities they were. Most were many miles from major roads and cities and all had their own character. When they planned their trip they made it a point to travel on rural secondary roads as much as possible. Lily remembered Bob saying something to the effect; if you want to see the truly interesting and beautiful part of America, travel the back roads and take your time. They were finding this to be so true. They came to a stop sign in the middle of this little town. The intersection was at the crossroads of two county roads. One went east and west and the other north and south. They had been driving north all day and when Lily turned left at this intersection to head west, Jacob said, "Mom I think you made a wrong turn back there. I thought we were heading north, toward Rawlins, Wyoming."

"I know son, I have a surprise for you."

"What do you mean a surprise, aren't we heading for Wyoming today?"

"Just trust me; I think you'll like it."

They drove for about 20 minutes, all the while gaining in elevation, and the forest got thicker and greener. They came to an intersection and Lily took out a piece of paper, studied it a second and turned right onto a gravel road.

"Mom, you're driving me crazy, where are we going?"

"Be patient, we're almost there."

They went a little over two miles on the gravel road when Lily pulled into a driveway with a gate. She got out, went to a tree and looked around for a second, picked up something and went to the gate and unlocked it. She opened the gait, drove through and locked it behind her. They drove about five hundred yards through the trees and came to an open area with the most gorgeous little rustic cabin, complete with a breathtaking, panoramic view. The cabin had a covered porch on all four sides and a bubbling, high mountain stream running only 40 feet from it. Jacob's mouth was open, and he said, "I can't believe this place Mom, what's going on?"

"This morning before you got up, Jess, Jack and I were setting at their kitchen table drinking coffee. Jess slid me this piece of paper with directions on it and proceeded to tell me about this cabin. It belongs to their family and Jack's brother's family. They all take turns using it and it was not going to be used by anyone until the weekend after next, so they offered it to us. In the trunk is a cooler with t-bone steaks and a lot of other wonderful goodies that they insisted we take. It's ours Jacob, and we can stay as long as we want. They both think a lot of you and wanted it to be a surprise. What do you think?"

"Oh my, mother, what a cool place! I can't wait to see inside and start exploring."

"What are we waiting for? Let's check it out."

Lily unlocked the door to the cabin and they slowly walked in. "This is amazing Jacob, look at that view and this wonderful fireplace."

"Where's the light switches, Mom?"

"Doesn't have any, we will have to use a kerosene lamp and do you see that pump by the sink, we pump our own water that comes from a spring and look at this a wood burning cook stove. I can't wait to use it. Jess told me all about it."

"Mom, this is truly amazing and I can't believe that some people who didn't even know us yesterday morning are letting us use it."

"I know what you mean; I think this is just a byproduct of meeting Bob's friends. He loved people who are kind and he loved helping people who needed it. I think we are going to experience the rewards of knowing him for a long time to come."

Lily and her son had a wonderful time exploring the cabin and everything around it. After some mishaps, extra smoke and ribbing from Jacob she was able to get the wood stove working good enough to fry some potatoes and two really good t-bones. After a wonderful meal they were sitting on the deck drinking tea and watching the sun go down. "I don't know which is more beautiful son, the sun going down here or on our desert. What do you think?"

"This is really nice Mom, but once a desert rat,

always a desert rat."

Lily laughed and said, "Well, I guess you're right, but I sure wouldn't mind spending a few days here every summer." Lily looked at Jacob with very serious eyes and said, "Do you really think Bob is with Jesus and we will see him again or what? Also, Jacob, if I died tonight do you think I would go to heaven? What do you think about all that stuff?"

"Those are pretty heavy questions for me to answer with a lot of authority. I mean it's not like I've been learning about God for years and years. I can tell you what has happened to me and what Bob and I talked about concerning all of this."

"That would be great, I couldn't ask for anything more."

"Let's see, you already know about Bob and me talking when we camped, and you know that I've been reading the Bible for the last few months. To be honest reading the Bible was interesting sometimes, but I was confused most of time. I told this to Bob the day before he died and he told me that was natural. He said once you actually accept Christ into your life it really opens up doors for understanding what God is telling us. I said I didn't understand that and he told me that the Bible is really the living Word of God. Living for real, not like a bug or plant, but alive in you. When you have God in you and you're reading His word everyday and making it part of your life, He helps you to understand things that you wouldn't have had a clue about before. And do you know what, Mom? He was right. When Bob gave me my Bible he told me to read the book of John first and I did. I re-read it after I accepted Him into my life, and I was amazed how much more sense it made. Does that make any sense to you?"

"Yea, I guess so, go on."

"Well, not only did I understand God's Word better, I felt something different after I accepted Him. I felt a peace that I've never experienced before. Bob told me that God will never leave us or forsake us and I feel that. I feel the security of really knowing He is there. I know one thing; I am very excited about learning more about Him and getting closer to Him. Mom, sometimes when I pray at night it seems like He's right there in my room with me. I don't know, I can't explain it very well."

"Jacob, this is amazing. The two people I love the most in my life have this relationship with God that I didn't even know could exist. I am excited and feel left out at the same time. What is the praying all about? I say a prayer once in awhile, usually when I am worried about you, but I have never really thought God would be listening to me much. I guess I said them in case you were in trouble or something. How do you pray to God? Is there a special way or something?"

"I asked Bob the same thing and he told me when I pray to go to a quiet place and talk to God like He is right there with me. He recommended that I start with thanking Him for everything that's on my heart. Then he told me he liked to praise God and he told me that will become easier as I got closer to Him. Then he told me to tell God what is on my heart and what I need help with. Mom, every day since I started really praying, I have prayed for you. I want you to find what I have. It's the most important thing in my life right now. I also know that having this relationship with Jesus has made it easier dealing with Bob's death."

Jacob looked away. His mom could see his eyes welling up and walked over to him and he stood up and they hugged. "Jacob, I love you so much. Please show me how to get this Christ of yours in my heart."

———————

They stayed in that quiet, serene place for two days. They took full advantage of no pressure, good food, and wonderful weather. They spent a lot of time studying and talking about what the Bible had to say to them. This quiet time together was something they had never had before. Lily realized that her little boy was growing up and she couldn't have been more pleased. When she prayed, she had no problem thinking of the blessing in her life to thank God for. She didn't know how long this wonderful sense of peace would last, but she was excited about the day they were in and what tomorrow would bring.

CHAPTER 23

For the next two days they took their time and wandered through towns with names like Rawlins, Muddy Gap, Lander, Riverton, Thermopolis, Worland, Greybull, and Shell. Most of them were small towns, and all of them had their own character and story to tell. The people they met were just ordinary folks just like them. In those two days they never meet one person that was rude or unwilling to answer their questions. Lily especially had grown to be very interested in the process of looking at person's face and eyes and wondering what they were all about. Wondering about the joy and the pain they had in their lives. What made them happy and what sorrows were they living with. Those two days gave them a peaceful time of reflection on their past and a time of looking deeper into the plans of their future and what it might hold.

The sign read "Lone Tree 33 miles." The first few days of their trip revolved around telling people about Bob's death and then sharing with these same people about their relationship with Bob. The last four days it had just been the two of them, and now it was time to meet Pat and Sammy. They were both apprehensive about this meeting. Lily had totally moved past the thoughts of jealousy and resentment toward them to the point of wanting to know them for who they might be as people and what it was like for them to be such a big part of Bob's life. Jacob felt the same way, to a degree, but also found himself somewhat infatuated with Sammy. He didn't have a clue what she was like or if she was even close to being as good looking as her picture. For all he knew she could be a selfish teenage brat who had gained a ton of weight and had a big pimple on her nose. They were about to find out. Lily had called Pat the day before and they had arranged a meeting at Pat and Sammy's home. They were expecting them and Lily wondered if they were as nervous as she was.

They found Pat and Sammy's house without any problems. It was a charming little place with a well manicured lawn and all the little touches of someone who cared for their home. As they were walking toward the front door, Lily said, "I am really nervous, how about you?"

"Yes I am. What if they don't like us or are not nice people or something?"

"I don't think that will be the case; let's find out."

Before Lily could knock on the door it opened, and a woman younger then she expected said, "You must be Lily and Jacob. I'm Pat and this is my daughter Samantha."

"Yes we are and I'm so glad to meet you."

As they were walking into the house, Lily looked at Jacob and could see the same surprised look on his face that she felt. Two things caught them somewhat off guard. Pat only had one arm and Samantha was a knock out. Jacob was thinking to himself that there was no way he was going to be able to talk to this girl. She had to be the most gorgeous thing he had ever seen. She was probably the most popular girl in her school, if not the whole state of Montana.

"Please have a seat," Pat said, "Can we offer you anything to drink, coffee or tea maybe?"

Lily said, "Not for me thanks."

Jacob mumbled something like, "I'm OK, thank you."

It was obvious that everyone was nervous and finally Pat said, "I am so sorry about Bob, I know he meant a lot to you two. When Annie York called and told us what happened and that you two might be coming to see us... well, I was excited and somewhat apprehensive at the same time. I just wanted to cry and morn him and not see anyone. Do you know what I mean?"

The ice had been broken. What Pat said and how she said it gave Lily a total sense of relief. She knew she would be able to trust this woman, even to the point of sharing her heart with her.

"I'm so glad you said that," Lily relied. "We've met several people on this journey, and I have to tell you I was the most nervous about meeting you."

"Well, don't be nervous any longer. We're glad you're here and I am very excited about hearing more about you two and your trip up here. As you no doubt know, Bob didn't talk much, especially about himself, but he did talk about you two and when he did, it was obvious that he cared a great deal for both of you."

"Bob talked to you about his life down in Denton?"

"Oh yes, we know about you and Jacob. You own a diner in Denton and you have a lady named Lucy working for you and a county deputy sheriff named Reilly. Is that right?"

"Yes that is right...but I have to be frank with you,

Bob didn't talk about his life up here in Lone Tree or any of the other people that we have met since we headed this way a week ago. Why is that, do you think? Why was he such a closed book around us? We didn't know anything about all of you folks until I found some 3x5 cards in his Bible with your names on them. Annie York knew about you and Sammy...or I mean Samantha."

Sammy smiled and said, "You can call me Sammy if you like. Bob is about the only one who did, I kind of liked it, mainly because he called me that ever since I was little. Kind of a personal thing between us I guess."

"I like Sammy too, and if you're sure you don't mind, that's what I would like to call you. I guess ever since Annie told me Bob called you that, it just stuck in my mind. But why didn't he tell us about all of these wonderful friends that he had? I don't understand. I didn't even know he had a son until Annie told me. Did you know about his son?"

Pat thought for a second and then said, "I know a few things and I don't know if any of them will make sense or are even correct. We all know Bob was a very private person. We only learned about some of his life away from Lone Tree in the last few years. One day he did tell me a little about his son, but only briefly. I could see the pain in his eyes and never pushed him on it at all. You have to understand that the relationship that Samantha and I had with Bob was different than I think you might have had. I considered Bob as my second dad and I think Samantha thought of him as a grandfather. To tell you the truth I think Bob loved you like a man would love a woman he would like to be married to and I think he thought of Jacob as a son. After thinking about it, I believe Bob was a little gun shy about getting any closer to you than he already was, because in his mind you would meet someone and marry and that would make him very happy for you, but it would also cause him to be extremely sad. I think he was scared to death that he would show up in Denton one day and you wouldn't have any need for him anymore. I know he was afraid that Jacob would lose interest in him and that bothered him a lot. The way he talked about you Jacob was something. You must be quite a nice young man. I know Samantha was excited that you were coming to visit us."

Sammy's face turned a little red and she said, "Mom you didn't need to say that."

"Well, it's true. After we got most of the crying out of us, we were both excited about meeting you. I know what kind of man Bob was and for him to care for someone as much as he did you two... well that says a lot about your character."

Lily had a sad and perplexed look on her face and she said, "I am so confused...could you tell me a little about your lives with Bob? Like did you do things together...you know what I mean, did you do family stuff with Bob?"

"As I said he was like a dad to me. I own a little café also and it has an apartment over it. We kept it set up just for Bob, but he was always over here for meals and gatherings of some kind. He went to church with us every Sunday and was part of a men's group there. Before Samantha got her driver's license he was always taking her and her friends places. My dad left me an old pick up and that became Bob's. He fixed that old thing up and it ran like a top. He would help me close the café and we would go for long walks and almost always I would talk and he would listen. It was always nice for us when he was here. When it got toward the end of summer and we knew he would be leaving pretty soon, it kind of bummed me out for awhile. I really loved him and would miss him terribly, but I knew he was excited to see you two again and that made it easier."

Lily felt the tears welling up in her and said, "Could I please use your bathroom and if it wouldn't be a bother I would love to take you up on that cup of coffee?"

Pat came back into the living with coffee and some sodas. Lily was still in the bathroom so Pat asked Jacob, "Is your mom all right? I'm not saying too much am I?"

"No, I don't think you are saying too much, you're telling us some things that we need to know. Please don't hold back, I really want to know as much as you will tell us. It makes me appreciate how lucky I was to have him in my life."

Lily came back into the room. It was obvious that she'd been crying and she said, "I am sorry, hearing about Bob's life up here really gave me a reality check. You see, you people treated Bob like he deserved to be treated. Down in Denton, Jacob and everyone else did also. Everyone, that is, except me. I need to tell you what happened the day before Bob died and that might help you understand why I'm feeling pretty low right now. I was behind the counter at the diner and I looked up and saw Bob standing outside the diner looking at me through a window. I hadn't seen him for several months and I was so excited to see him that I ran outside and hugged him and then I kissed him on the lips. I had never done that before and I was little embarrassed. I couldn't believe how glad I was to see him. Anyway, later that evening a couple roughnecks were in the diner and one of them was saying some things to put Bob down and it made me mad and I ran them off. It really shook me up, so Bob came to me and had me sit down. He proceeded to make me a cup of tea and help me put everything into perspective. Then he did something I will remember for the rest of my life. He locked up the diner, closed the blinds and put some money in the jute box. He then came over and asked me to dance. I remember it so clearly. The first thing that came to my mind was what if someone saw us dancing? What if someone saw me dancing with a transient? Then it struck me like a lightning bolt, I was treating Bob just like those two idiots were. Oh, I might have treated him fair and square and all that stuff but I knew right then that I had been telling Bob with my eyes all of those years that he wasn't good enough for me. I danced two dances with him and realized how much I loved him and that I was going to do whatever it took to make it up to him. You say Bob had meals in your house all the time, well I had many meals with Bob at our diner, but I never once had him over for dinner at our house...not once."

Lily bent over and with her face in her hands she wept almost uncontrollably.

Jacob who was sitting next to his mom, put his arm around her and said, "We knew that this process was going to be tough, but I have to tell you something. You know how much I loved Bob, but to be honest I'm a little mad at him right now."

Lily stopped sobbing and looked at him and said, "Why would you be mad at Bob?"

"I can understand why Bob was a little distant with you. He didn't want to lose you, but in doing that he never showed you the whole Bob. Up here, and in Elmira and Bolt, he was just Bob. In Denton he was probably so insecure with you he never gave you anything to grab a hold of. You say you didn't treat him like he deserved to be treated. I think you didn't treat him like family because he was afraid to let you into his world. If he would have opened up to you a little more, it would have made him more vulnerable to getting hurt. He never took the chance, always waiting for you to make the first move and when you kissed him the day before he died, that was the move he was waiting for. If he would have been more aggressive from the beginning it might have been different. I'm sure in his mind, though, if he was more aggressive you would probably run him off and he didn't want to take the chance. We will never know, but I do know you shouldn't beat yourself up about it."

"What an astute young man you are, "Pat said. "That makes a lot of sense; and I think you're right. I remember one time Bob was telling me what a wonderful woman you are and I said to him why don't you court her and get a ring on her finger? You know what he told me? He said that would be nice but if he did that it would scare you to death and it would ruin the trust you had in him. I think Jacob is right on the mark, we may never know, but you definitely should go a little easier on yourself."

Lily sat up straight and with a slight smile on her face said, "Thank you, both of you. That does give me some solace, and I promised myself I wouldn't be all sappy on this trip and I am not going to be. Forgive me; I do feel a lot better getting this all out in open."

"That's great because you had both me and Samantha crying again. So instead of crying what do you think about having a nice lunch?"

Lily laughed and said, "I would love that and I know Jacob must be hungry."

"OK, we have two choices. We have plenty of food here or we could go over to our café. Either way is fine with us. What do you think?"

"It seems like I've been all wrapped up in myself every since we got here. I would love to know about your café and family, and anything else you would share with us."

"OK then, let's go down to the good ole Lone Tree Café and see what we can scare up."

They decided to walk to the café and on the way, and during lunch, Pat told them how she'd come to own the café by inheriting it from her folks. She also explained how she lost her arm in a farming accident, and about how her husband was killed when his load of hay on a big semi shifted and he lost control and hit a tree when Samantha was only three. They were almost finished with lunch when Lily said, "Annie told us you recently got married and how happy Bob was with him. Please tell us about your husband."

"That's an interesting story. After I lost my first husband I was pretty down for several years. I had it in my mind that no one would ever be interested in a one armed waitress with a little kid. After Bob was around for awhile I started pulling out of that frame of mind. Bob was such an encourager. He became my friend, dad, and sounding board and he was so good with Samantha. He loved her so much and when she was little he fussed over her more than I did. Anyway, I started feeling a lot better about myself and the possibility of marriage someday. But, to be honest, the pickin's for a good husband around here are pretty slim. Bob had become close friends with our pastor, Tony Largo. I hope you have time to meet him, he's a wonderful man. When Bob wasn't helping me, or someone else around here, he was out at Tony and his wife Janet's little ranch. They have a place a few miles from town with cattle and horses. Bob loved it out there and he really liked Tony and Janet. A couple years ago, their son Chris retired from the military and moved home. Here's this guy who's 38 years old, never been married, traveled all over the world and chooses to move back to this little town. I know the main reason he came back is for his parents. He is just that kind of guy. Chris and Bob hit it off wonderfully. They both had seen combat in the military, and as far as I know Chris is the only one Bob ever talked to about his time in Vietnam. Chris is a lot like Bob, he is a quiet, none assuming type of guy. Do anything for anybody, but shy, very shy. He was home for close to six months before he would say more than two words in a row to me. To make a long story short, because of Bob and his subtle ways, Chris started to come out of his shell and he finally asked me out on date and the rest is history. He is out at the ranch right now and will be in around six. I would love for you to meet him."

"Was Bob here when you got married?"

"Oh yes, Chris asked me to marry him at Christmas time last year and I, of course, said yes. We decided to wait until Bob was here so he could give me away. That was important to both of us. It was a wonderful wedding. I will show you pictures later if you like."

"I would like that very much."

"When Annie called, and told us about the accident, it really shook Samantha and I up. Chris was right there for both of us and I knew it bothered him a lot also. I didn't know how much, until a few days ago we were all out at the ranch. Chris was standing over by the corrals looking out toward the horses and the mountains. He didn't hear me walk up to him and I kind of took him by surprise. He'd been crying, and when I asked what was wrong, he said that he and Bob would stand there and talk and that was never going to happen again. He hugged me and he said, Patty I didn't realize how much I loved that guy. I said me to and we had a good cry together."

Lily had been glancing at Sammy while Pat talked and noticed several times her dabbing her eyes. Here was this beautiful young woman and it was obvious that Bob had an impact on her life also. With a gentle smile Lily said, "Sammy would you mind telling us something about Bob that comes to your mind?"

With a surprised and somewhat embarrassed look on her face Sammy squirmed a little and said, "Wow, there is so much I could say." She thought a second, and then with a beautiful smile that flamed the fire that was already melting Jacob's heart, she said, "When I was 12 years old, we were preparing to go on a youth group camping trip. I had gone on the two previous years and liked it OK. It wasn't great, but OK. Anyway, the day before we were to leave, one of the couples taking us had an emergency and weren't going to be able to go. Our youth pastor and his wife told us if they didn't find someone else to take their place we would have to cancel. They tried to find someone and couldn't, and when they called mom to tell her they were going to have to cancel, she said I can't speak for him but have you thought of asking Bob? He said let me think about it and 15 minutes later he was at the café to talk to Bob. He asked Bob, and Bob looked at my mom and she smiled and told him it would be great for him and the kids. The next morning we loaded up his old pickup with all the gear and we went camping. It was great; we all had more fun than we ever had before. Bob taught us all kinds of stuff. The youth pastor and his wife were totally mesmerized by everything Bob taught us. He also could tell the best campfire stories we ever heard. He just made everything so fun and interesting. Usually we were ready to go home after one night, but with Bob there, we didn't want to leave after three nights and days. The next year we all made sure Bob was going along before it was time to go. The amount of kids and adults who went doubled from the year before. Bob, me, and my best friend ended up leaving a day early with all the gear and tents and had everything set up when the rest of the group got there the next day. That first night was magical for my friend and me. We had Bob all to ourselves. Instead of telling us stories he got us talking about ourselves and what we wanted out of life, then how we were going go about getting it. I was 13 and felt like I had the world by the tail. The next year was just as good. Everything went perfect; everyone had a great time, but after we got back Satan raised his ugly head."

"What do mean, what happened?" Lily asked.

"Well, a lady from another church made a big deal to our pastor about Bob being with my friend and me alone for one night before everyone else came. She made a big issue out of someone who was almost a stranger being with two girls by himself. Pastor Tony defended Bob, but the lady told him that if he continued to allow this to happen she would contact the state children services office and ask for an investigation of the whole deal but especially Bob. When Pastor Tony talked to Bob about it, Bob just calmly told him that if this was to go on, no one would win. He said there would be rumors and people wouldn't understand and they'd draw the wrong conclusions. He said if they really needed him, he would go up when everyone else did, but he thought it best he just bow out. Bob just didn't want to cause any problems for anyone. I don't think he ever realized how much we liked him there with us. Anyway I quit going a few years ago."

"Did you ever go camping together again?" Jacob asked.

"Oh yes, we went two or three times with mom, Pastor Tony and Janet, and we always took one or two of my friends."

"You went with them too?" Lily asked Pat.

"It was fun, we ate like kings and played games and told stories. I was never crazy about not having hot water and a shower and all of that stuff, but for two or three days it was great. Let's head back to the house and figure out what to make for supper tonight."

Lily and Jacob stayed in Lone Tree that night and had a very pleasant time with Pat and Sammy. They met and got to know Chris and his parents and fell in love with all of them. They all were kind and down to earth people. It was easy to see why Bob would enjoy spending his summers here. They talked about Bob's wishes to set up a small scholarship fund for the kid's education. They even produced a little brochure explaining The Bob Dolan scholarship fund to give to people who knew him. Jacob and Sammy went for a long walk together and got to know each other. The next morning as they were getting ready to leave, Pat came to Lily and Jacob and told them that Samantha, Chris and her had talked and wanted to invite Jacob to come up for the whole summer if he wanted. He could work on the ranch with Chris. Jacob's eyes got huge and he said, "That would be so cool, I would love to do that."

Pat said, "Don't give us an answer now, you and your mom talk about it and let us know in a week or so."

Lily smiled and said, "I've got a feeling we will be talking about it right away, thank you so much for the offer. I guess we better head for Oregon, what do you think Jacob?"

"I suppose we should, but I sure like it here."

"I do too, but we have a long way to go and I know we need to get back to Denton pretty soon."

Pat said, "Two years ago we took off for a couple weeks to spend on the Oregon Coast and on the way we stopped for a couple hours in this little town called Gooding, in Idaho. They have this little café that has a very exciting program that I think you might be interested in. It is called Reaching Out and I am pretty sure you will be impressed. Ask someone there about their program and how it's run. I think you will be glad you did."

"We're headed for Yellowstone National Park today and will be in Idaho tomorrow, do you know if Gooding is on our way?"

Pat showed them where it was on a map and it worked perfectly for them to stop there for lunch. Everyone hugged each other and Lily and Jacob were back on the road.

CHAPTER 24

The drive west was wonderful. They got to Yellowstone in time to drive through the park. They saw buffalo, elk, coyotes, and they thought they saw a glimpse of a grizzly bear. After spending some time at Old Faithful they continued west. They decided to drive all the way to Blackfoot, Idaho before they got a room. It took several hours to get there but they had plenty to talk about. Lily had Annie York and Bob's son in River Bend on her mind and Jacob didn't stray too far from talking about Sammy and going back to Lone Tree for the summer.

The final few miles into Gooding, Idaho, the next morning was dotted with small farms and ranches. Some had cattle and horses with corn and alfalfa fields, while others had potatoes and beans. "I really like this country don't you?" Lily said.

"Yeah, it's OK, but I like Lone Tree better."

"I wonder if a little gal by the name of Samantha has anything to do with that preference."

Jacob laughed and said, "Maybe just a little."

"I'm not hungry yet, what say we find this Reaching Out place that Pat wanted us to see and have a something to drink, and then keep on moving. What do you think?"

"That sounds good to me; I'm not very hungry either."

Gooding was a nice little town like so many others they had seen in the last few days. They had no problem finding The Reaching Out Café as the town only had one main street. They walked into the little place and an attractive women who was probably in her forties, greeted them, "Good morning, how are you folks this morning?"

"We're doing real good, thank you," Lily replied.

"We just opened and you're our first customers, I hope you're hungry, we have meat loaf or chicken and rice today."

Lily studied her face and said, "To tell you the truth we're not very hungry right now. The main reason we stopped was because a friend over in Montana told us we should see your place, but she didn't tell us why. She just said she thought we'd be glad we did. Does that make any sense?"

The lady smiled and said, "I'm glad to know that people as far away as Montana are sending customers our way. That's encouraging! Yes, I do think I know why your friend recommended you stop by. We won't be busy for about fifteen minutes, would you like something to drink and I will tell about our little café?"

"That would be nice, I'll have a cup of coffee, black. Jacob do you want something?"

"A Coke or Pepsi, please."

"Have a seat, I'll be right back."

The women returned with their drinks and said, "My name is Debby, where are you folks from?"

"My name is Lily and this is my son Jacob, and we are from Denton, Arizona. It's nice to meet you. I appreciate you taking the time to talk to us."

"Oh, it's my pleasure, I love telling people about what is going on in this place. I'll give you a brief description of what we're all about and then, if it doesn't get too busy, I'll answer any questions you might have. We're a non-profit organization whose main goal is to provide a hot meal for anyone who might not be able to afford it otherwise. We also have a goal of providing a place where people meet and have a meal and see and interact with people that they would normally never see or talk to. We're open from 11 to 3 Monday through Saturday. Everyone who works here is a volunteer and about 60% of our food is donated. We have a suggested price of $1.50 per meal. About a third of our customers get a meal at no cost. Another third pay the $1.50 and the final third pay more. We average about 100 meals a day and we have everyone from doctors and lawyers to transients coming in. We've only been open three years, but every year it gets better. The interaction we see between people of totally different economic and social classes is exciting. The whole process is contagious and it has made our community much more closely knit. I could go on and on about what it has done for our community, but I let you ask any questions you might have instead."

"Well, I have to say I'm impressed. I have so many questions, but the one that comes to mind first is, do you have trouble getting enough volunteers?"

"We were worried about that at first, but it's proven not to be a problem, but a blessing. The volunteers get a lot out of being here, in many ways. Back in the kitchen are Gus, Robert and Jerry and they have been here since we opened. Betty, Fran, Peggy, Sheri, and Paula have also been here from the beginning. Whenever one of us can't be here, we have a long list of people who will fill in. In the summer, and on Saturdays, we get a lot of help from high school kids. Unfortunately, we lost one of our most important people a few months ago. His name was Danny and he went home to the Lord. He was our, 'go to guy.' He picked up and delivered all of our food and supplies and supervised the maintenance on the building. It's taken two people to fill his shoes, we really miss him."

"Sounds like it's a church type of deal."

"No, we're not part of any church. Almost all of the volunteers are Christians, but that's not a requirement for working or eating here."

People started coming in and Debby had to greet them. After greeting the third group in a row she said to Lily and Jacob, "Which way are you folks headed?"

"We're going to River Bend in Oregon."

"I'll tell you what, if you're really interested in this concept, the lady who got us started runs a similar place in Boise. It's less than two hours from here and easy to find. Her name is Carolyn, and if you leave now you'll get there after their noon rush. I know she would be glad to share how this all works."

Lily looked at Jacob and said, "That would be perfect. I would like to know more, what do you think?"

Jacob smiled and said, "I can see your wheels turning Mom, that's fine with me."

Debby looked at Jacob and said, "I have a feeling that your mom is a very kind, is that right?"

"Yes, she sure is."

"Let me go to my office and I'll get you Carolyn's card and directions on how to get there."

"She seems like a very nice lady, doesn't she Mom?"

"Yes, she does, I bet all of these people are pretty cool."

Debby came back with a card and said, "Please make sure to stop and see Carolyn, she is quite a gal. You'll like her."

"We will, and I want to thank you for taking time for us and for what all of you do here. I'm impressed."

Debby gave them both a hug and said, "I hope you have a safe trip. It has been a pleasure to meet both of you."

The 100 mile drive to Boise went by quickly and they had no problem finding the Boise Reaching Out Café. It was considerably larger than the café in Gooding, and like Gooding, it was in excellent shape. It was obvious that they took a lot of time to make their building look as nice and clean as they possibly could. When they walked into the café at 1:45 that afternoon there were about thirty people eating lunch. They were greeted by a very attractive older woman. "Good afternoon folks, hope you're hungry, we have a great turkey dinner or spaghetti and meat balls."

"Yes, we are hungry, but we would also like to speak with Carolyn if possible."

"You must be the folks from Arizona. Debby called me and said you might be stopping by. I'm Carolyn."

"Yes we are. My name is Lily and this is my son Jacob. For some reason we are suppose to talk to you. Two days ago we had never even heard of Reaching Out and now we are here. I guess God has something in mind, I'm not sure what, but hopefully we'll find out today."

"I would like to suggest that you have a nice lunch and when you're through I will ask someone to cover for me up here and we can go into my office and, hopefully, we can figure out what God has in mind. Would that be OK?"

"That's perfect; I'm really looking forward to the lunch and talking to you."

Lily had the turkey and Jacob had spaghetti. The food was just like home cooking and everyone treated them like royalty. But it wasn't just them, everyone was treated like they were long lost friends. Besides the food and service being great, there was a warm feeling about the place. One table had four very well dressed ladies eating and having a nice conversation. Another table had two men in suits eating and talking with two men who were obviously down on their luck. The atmosphere was amazing. Lily could only imagine what it was like during the rush hour.

After they were finished eating Carolyn came to their table with another lady and introduced her as Karen.

"Glad to meet you, Lily said, I just love your food and how comfortable this place feels."

"I am glad to meet both of you too, this is a nice place to eat and maybe meet someone new in your life. I'm glad you are here. Carolyn told me you are from Arizona and that you are going back to her office to chat about Reaching Out. Would you like a refill on your drinks before you go back?"

Both Lily and Jacob declined any more to drink and they followed Carolyn back to her office. "Please have a seat," Carolyn said. "I know Debby told you a little bit about what we do, so why don't we start off by you just asking me any questions you might have and we can go from there?"

Lily smiled at this wonderfully composed and gentle woman and said, "To tell you the truth Carolyn, I'm not sure why we are here. A friend recommended we stop in Gooding to visit Reaching Out and that she was sure we would be glad we did. I'm tremendously impressed with what all of you people are doing but we live in a very small town in Arizona and Jacob and I own a little diner there. Our town is so small that we really do not have any people having a problem getting a hot meal. Once in awhile we get someone passing through that is having a tough time. They don't stay very long because there is nothing there for them. I would love to know more about what you do and how it all works but I am not sure how it could be applicable to our little town."

"I understand what you're saying. Let me give you kind of an outline of our whole program, and maybe something we do here might fit. Percentage wise, we are real close to what Gooding does, except because of our size we serve about 400 meals per day. Also, because of the size of our building, we're able to provide some additional services that places like Gooding can't. For instance, Karen, the gal you met before we came back here, runs a counseling program for pregnant women. She has partnered with a dear friend by the name of Vicki and they provide counseling for women who are pregnant and struggling on whether or not to have an abortion. They don't beat them over the head with the Bible or put them through guilt trips or any of that kind of stuff. They simply make sure that these women know all of the options they have available to them. You would be amazed how many success stories have come out of that little office over the years.

We also have a program that is run by a group of professional and business people to simply give free advice on everything from starting a new business to legal matters. That group consists of accountants, lawyers, career advisors, and business managers. They are here for four hours on the first and third Wednesday of every month. It's not unusual for them to help 50 clients on one of those days. Let's see, oh yes, we had a local church burn down a few years ago and they now meet in our dining room every Saturday night and Sunday morning. It's worked so well that they're not planning to rebuild. The same atmosphere we have here at lunch time they have in that church. They reach out to everyone and it has proven to be a very successful ministry. In fact they have more than doubled the amount of people attending as when they had a nice church building. I could go on and on, but does any of that strike a chord?"

Lily's was thinking about everything she had said and like a light bulb going on she said, "If you don't mind I would like to share something with you that I would normally not talk about to someone I just met."

"Please do, I'm here for you as long as you need me."

"Where do I start and not make this into a long story? The week before last, a very dear man in Jacobs and my lives died in an accident. This man would spend his winters with us in Arizona and in the summer time he was with another family in Montana. Like I said he was a very special man. Anyway, two days after his service Jacob and I left on a journey. You see, he had this wonderful old Bible he'd been carrying around for the 15 years we'd known him. When I went through that Bible I found several 3x5 cards with people's names on them and the towns they lived in. We have been to all of those towns except for one, and that is where we're heading now. In this process we've met some very wonderful people. Also during this trip I accepted Jesus as my Lord and Savior and Jacob did the same thing the day before our friend died. This whole thing has been a real whirlwind for us and what comes to mind after listening to you tell me about what goes on here, I think God might want us to establish a place where people in our little town can have church. The closest church to us is over 20 miles away, and I think there are a lot of folks who would come if we had something closer. Our diner is pretty small, but I know we could seat at least 50 people if we stretched a little. I don't know, maybe that's why were suppose to meet you."

"I know one thing for sure; it is real exciting that you both have come to know Christ. That makes my day! It really does. Let me tell you a little more about the church that meets here. Because their expenses have decreased so much by not having to maintain their old church they are able to have three full time pastors on staff. They also have established two satellite churches. One west of here and one to the north. Both of these little towns, which sound very similar to yours, meet in buildings other than a conventional church building. One group meets in a small café like yours and one in the hall of their volunteer fire department. You can imagine the opposition they had to that. After several town hall type meetings they were able to get approval to use it and it has worked out very well, both for the church and the fire hall. So, these three pastors rotate through the three churches by spending one month at a time in each of them. It caused a little bit of a problem in that one man is not at the same place all the time however, the benefits have far outweighed the negatives. All three pastors have nice offices in this building and one dynamite secretary that takes care of all of them. They don't compete against each other; instead they work as a team and draw strength from each other. They have established some amazing outreach ministries and we're excited about how well it has gone. Twice a year all three churches meet here and I have to tell you, this place is packed out on those two Sundays. Our governor and our major have both attended to those services several times. It's all about community and working together. Maybe they have some advice for you that would make it feasible for you do something similar."

"Wow," Lily said with excitement in her voice, "That

is interesting. I think we could do something like that, but I don't have a clue where to start."

"Before you leave, I'll get you the numbers of several people who would be more than happy to share with you how it has worked for them. Lily, what town do you live in Arizona and would you mind me asking the name of your friend who died and how he died?"

"I don't mind at all, we live in Denton and our friend died in a fire while he was saving two little kids, and his name was Bob Dolan. Why do you ask?"

"You might not believe this, but I have dinner every Thursday night with my brother-in-law, Joseph, and his family. Last Thursday he was obviously bummed out about something, and when I asked him why, he told me he'd just found out that an old army buddy who had saved his life in Vietnam had died in a tragic accident in Arizona. He also said he died in the process of saving two little kids and I think he said his name was Dolan. I don't think this a coincidence; they must be the one and the same. My brother-in-law said his friend was from River Bend in Oregon and he'd lost contact with him several years ago. He tried to find him several times, but he said it was like he dropped off the face of the earth."

"River Bend is the last town on our list. Bob was from River Bend and he left there about 16 years ago. It has to be the same man." Lily said.

"Oh my, I wish Joseph was here. He's at a medical convention in Chicago and won't be back until the day after tomorrow. I know he would so like to meet you and learn more about what Mr. Dolan has been doing all of these years."

"Bob was such a private person; he never talked about his time in the military or hardly anything else in his past. Did your brother-in-law tell you anything about what happened in Vietnam?"

"Yes, he did. Joseph was a wet behind the ears 2nd Lieutenant leading a squad of Special Forces men that did a lot of covert stuff. He told us that before he took charge of this unit his CO told him if he wanted any chance of staying alive he would be wise to listen to everything Sgt. Dolan told him. He was on his second tour of duty in Vietnam and Joseph was lucky he had him. Anyway, he had only been there about a month when they were doing some spy stuff, I think he call it recon. There were twelve men in his squad and they had been behind enemy lines for three days trying to find a supply or ammo depot or something like that. They were successful in gathering all the information they needed and were headed out when they were ambushed. They were to be picked up by helicopters less than a half mile from where they started taking enemy fire. Joseph told us he was scared to death and not real sure what to do. He looked at Sgt. Dolan and the Sgt., without hesitation, told him to get the squad running for the pickup location as soon as he gave him the signal. The signal was real simple; Sgt. Dolan and a corporal name Varin stood up and started blasting away. The enemy was surprised, and it bought Joseph and nine others enough time to get on their way to the landing zone, or so he thought. Joseph had gone about two hundred yards and was behind his men when he took a bullet in the back and went down. He woke up two days later in a MASH unit. He learned that Sgt. Dolan found him on his way to the landing zone and carried him all the way to the helicopter. Apparently there was a lot of return fire from our boys at the landing zone, but the enemy just kept firing away. After Sgt. Dolan got Joseph to the helicopter, he shouted "one more" at the pilot, "don't leave." He ran back toward enemy fire and was able to carry another man, who had also been shot in the back and couldn't move, to the helicopter. As soon as he got him in, Sgt. Dolan collapsed on the ground and they had to throw him in before they could leave. When they got him to the MASH unit they found scrap metal in his back, right next to his spinal cord, and he'd been shot in his leg and shoulder. Both Joseph and your Bob were sent back to the states and Bob ended being discharged a few months later. Joseph said they were not able to get the scrap metal of Bob's back, so he would get a small disability check for the rest of his life. They kept in contact with each other for several years and then nothing, until now."

"I had no idea," Lily said, "I knew his back gave him problems sometimes, but he never told me why. One more piece of the puzzle of Bob's past put into place. Yet another reason I'm so glad we stopped to see you."

There was a knock on the office door and Karen opened it and said, "Carolyn I am sorry to bother you but we have an incident out front with a couple drunks who want money instead of food."

"Would you please excuse me for a few minutes, I'll be right back."

Karen stayed with them and said, "Sorry about that, these type of things happen once in awhile. Where in Arizona are you folks from?"

"We're from Denton, and on our way to River Bend, Oregon."

"It's none of my business, but I bet Carolyn hasn't told you the whole story about why this program is so successful. I like to blow her horn sometimes because she never does. Everything we do here is a team effort but Carolyn and Jesus are the glue that keeps it all running.

She started this program ten years ago almost totally by herself. It was terribly difficult at first and I know her husband was waiting for her to give up and move on. When she wouldn't give up, her husband and his brother got behind her with some help from some politicians. She was tireless in putting this together and it just keeps growing. There are 13 Reaching Out Cafes in three different states that all got their start from here, and she is the reason. I'm telling you this because I know she won't. Two years ago, she was named woman of the year for the whole state of Idaho, and last year she had dinner at the White House because of her work. Yet she is so humble. It's not unusual to find her down here at night scrubbing floors or doing paper work. Her husband and his brother were very successful surgeons here in Boise. He was a great guy, but he died in a mountain climbing accident several years ago. She sure doesn't need to be down here almost every day. She is a successful author and involved in several other community and church projects. She's an amazing woman. Anyway I am real proud to have her as my friend and I thought I would tell you those things. Don't tell her I told you or she will be mad at me."

"Thank you Karen for telling us that. Sometimes it is important to acknowledge people like her. That's kind of what we are doing for a friend of ours. What kind of writing does she do?"

"Oh, she started with a novel about a high school romance and then an excellent book on her husband's life and how God got her through his death. Right now she is working on a project she is involved in with an orphanage in The Sudan."

"How impressive, was the high school romance about her?"

"I don't think so. We were friends in high school and I knew her first love and he is not like the guy in her book. Her boyfriend in high school was kind of a meat ball. Couldn't handle the booze. Good looking thought. The guy in her book was more what I think her husband would have been like."

Carolyn came back into the office and said, "Sorry about that, those two men had a hard time understanding why they shouldn't get the money for two free meals that they didn't eat. While I was talking to them Eddy and James came out and they understood a lot better and left. Never a dull moment around here, right Karen?"

"That's for sure and that's why we love it. Nice meeting both of you, and I hope we meet again."

Karen left and Lily said, "I will probably never know all the benefits of stopping and talking to you today, so all I'm going to say is, I thank you from the bottom of my heart for your time and for what you do. We will be in touch with your church people. I also have a little brochure on an educational trust fund we have set up in Bob's name, if you want to give it to your brother-in-law. You can also tell him that someday we plan to put together a book or something about Bob's life and if we keep in touch, I will let you know more about it."

"I will give Joseph this and I know he will be pleased that we met. I'm sure we will be talking more in the future."

They all hugged and said their good-byes and Lily and Jacob were back on the road headed west.

CHAPTER 25

They decided to head for La Grande, Oregon. They wouldn't get there until late in the day but it put them less than 200 miles from River Bend. Another café and motel, and then the next day they would meet Annie York for lunch and Bob's son and his family at five in the afternoon.

The last hour of driving toward River Bend the freeway ran alongside the mighty Columbia River and they were both in awe of how big it was and the beauty of the land around it. "You know, son, we have seen some of the most amazing country since we left Denton. I can understand why Bob enjoyed it so much."

"I know, Mom, and can you imagine how he saw it? The distance we've gone this morning probably took him a week. I can only envision what he saw and the people he met."

"We're close to meeting some people who were a real secret in his life. I don't have a clue how this meeting with Annie and Bob's son is going to go, but I'm excited about heading home as soon as we are done. How about you?"

"I know exactly what you mean. This trip has been a whirlwind of joy and sadness and great people and beautiful country, but I'm ready to be home again and start our new life, whatever that might be."

They found the law office of York & York and parked

across the street. They said a quick prayer and entered the office. A very pleasant receptionist was behind the front desk. "Hello, can I help you?" she asked.

"My name is Lily Fields and this is my son Jacob, we're a little early, but we have an appointment with Annie York."

"Annie is expecting you, please follow me."

They followed the receptionist down a short hallway to an office with the door opened. "Annie, Miss Fields and her son Jacob are here."

The receptionist went back to her desk and a very attractive woman who was probably in her fifty's came to them and said, "I am so thankful you are arrived safely." She shook Jacob's hand and said, "Jacob, I am so glad to meet you."

She then took both of Lily's hands in hers, looked in her eyes for a second, and then gave her a hug. "It's so nice to finally meet both of you, please have a seat." Annie closed the door and said, "Anna has prepared a lunch for us in here. I hope you don't mind, I thought it would give us more privacy."

A beautiful antique maple table with four matching chairs around it had a banquet of delicate sandwiches, salads, fruit, and drinks. Lily looked at all the food on the table and said, "Annie this is wonderful. You shouldn't have gone to all this trouble."

"It was no trouble at all, at least not for me. I was just going to have pop and pizza. Anna did all of this. I will tell you more later, but Bob meant a great deal to Anna and she wanted to do this for you two. So we have as much time as you want and please don't hesitate, enjoy this food. I thought we could talk and eat at the same time. Two things that I enjoy, sometimes I over indulge in both areas."

"I know what you mean, I'm the same way." Lily said.

All three of them prepared a plate of food. Annie sat behind her desk, Lily set in a very comfortable chair by the corner of the desk and Jacob sat at the table with all the food. Annie ate a grape and then said, "I've been thinking about this meeting with you two for several days, and I decided I would just tell you my part of the story and we can go from there. Would that be all right?"

"That's perfect, especially since we get to enjoy this food while you talk." Lily responded.

"Many years ago, I met my husband Dennis while attending law school in Portland. It was our last year of school and we fell madly in love. We got married one month before we both passed the bar exams. Dennis was born and raised in River Bend and I grew up in Gresham, which is only about 70 miles west of here. We decided to set up our law practice here in River Bend. We really went out on a limb and put our shingle out as York & York at this very location. Because Dennis was already so well-known here, our practice grew and we have done well. Bob was also raised here, and when he got out of college he started a construction and land development company from scratch. He and Dennis were in the same graduating class from River Bend High School. They were friends, but not close friends. Anyway, Bob had been in business for three years before we started our practice and was making a name for himself. He started out very small and just kept building his business up as he went. By the time we got here, Bob had four men working for him and some excavation equipment. Bob was Dennis's first client. He wanted to develop a small piece of land and Dennis helped him put it together. About five years after we came here Dennis started leaning more and more toward defense work. He liked being in a trial setting and even though I was OK with trial work, he liked it better. We slowly evolved into me handling most of the common law work and Dennis concentrated on defense cases. Because of this, Bob became my client. I got to know him through the work I did for him and we also went to the same church and served on some community boards and committees at the same time. He married Anita and they had a son and everything was going well. Then things started to change for Dennis and me. I wasn't able to have children, and I think that might have been part of our problems. Dennis started drinking and we just seemed to drift in two different directions over the years. One day Bob was in this very office, and we were discussing a project he wanted to do. I remember it was getting late in the afternoon, and he said he'd better get going so I could get out of here. I told him that wasn't a problem and that I would probably be here for a few more hours anyway. He said something about me being home for Dennis and in a state of self pity I said something like, Dennis could care less when I got home I know that took Bob by surprise and I could tell it concerned him. Then he surprised me back, and said he knew exactly how I felt and then left anyway and went back to his office."

Lily had finished a sandwich and she said, "How old was their son at that time?"

"Oh, let's see, he was probably six or seven. That afternoon started kind of a dialog over the next few years where we would say things to each other that made it evident that things were not as good as they should be in our home lives. Dennis, even though he was drinking too much, became a very good defense attorney and my practice was doing well also. Bob kept building up his business and two years before he left he had over 20 employees. He was always using his assets for church and community projects and was literally a workaholic. One day he came in to talk to me about a large project that was somewhat complicated. He had been approached by a local real estate agent who had inherited a very nice 50 acre parcel of land. Adjoining those 50 acres was a 350 acre piece that was for sale at a fair price. The real estate agent's name was Morgan and what he proposed to Bob was for them to go together and buy the 350 acres, and then do a first class subdivision using both pieces of land. The zoning was five acre minimum and almost all of the property had a gorgeous view of a big valley and a breathtaking view of Mt. Hood. Morgan needed someone like Bob because he didn't have the financial strength to put it all together and Bob did. Anyway Bob did all of the necessary groundwork to make sure it was a good idea, because it was going to be a huge financial commitment on his part. Morgan was putting up the 50 acres and that's it. The income potential was significant and they proceeded to go through with it. Before he signed the contract to buy the 350 acres he brought the contract into me to check out. Everything was in order and before he left he asked me my gut feeling on the whole deal. I knew he was in a position to make several million dollars on the term of the project, but that is not what he was asking. I told him I did not think too much of Morgan but Bob had put himself in the position of calling all the shots. I asked him if he had thought about buying the 350 by himself and he said he would never do that to Morgan or anyone else. I told him as far as I could see he had covered all of the bases. They had received approval from all of the agencies involved and a final sign off by the county planning commission. Morgan had several buyers lined up and they went ahead and bought the land. Then one

Friday afternoon everything started to go bad. We later called that day 'Black Friday'. They were scheduled to have a big ground breaking ceremony the following Monday, but shortly after lunch on that black Friday a courier delivered a packet to this office. It was the copy of a petition to the court to stop the subdivision. It was filed by an environmental group out of Portland. The planning commission had three separate public meetings to make sure all bases were covered. This group had been represented by an attorney at all three meetings. They objected to the project, but they didn't have a leg to stand on, and they knew it. Anyway, they filed this petition on the grounds that there was new potential evidence that the land in question was the habitat of speckled owls, which were on the endanger species list. Later that afternoon, we received a directive from the court to not proceed with the development until after a hearing that was scheduled for three weeks from that date. I contacted Bob as soon as I got the petition and he was in my office when the directive from the court arrived. I remember it so well. Bob was very calm and he asked me if they really could hold them up and for how long. We knew it was a scam, because Bob went to great lengths with Fish and Wildlife people to make sure nothing like this could happen. I told him that they could throw a wrench into the works for awhile, but I didn't know for how long. When word got out a whole lot of people were upset. The county had those two pieces of property on the tax roles for less than $500,000 and they had estimated that after the project was completed it would be in the 20 million range, so it was a big deal for the county. No less than 60 people were going to be employed for a considerable amount of time. It was a big deal for a lot of people. Bob had not bid on any jobs because they were going to start on this project. It looked bad, and it was, and it got worse.

They were able to hold up the whole project for fourteen months, all on a scam. By the time the door was opened again it was too late. Interest rates had climbed to over 12% and one of our major employers in this area closed their doors. Everything had fallen apart for Bob and his business, but Bob was a fighter and I knew he could pull out of it. The land deal is not what broke him, that happened at home. Everything I am telling you is pretty much public knowledge so I don't think Bob would mind me telling you all of this. I knew that things at home were not going well for a long time and this just made it worse.

Lily with anger in her voice said, "That is the same as a crime to me, how did they get away with doing something like that and didn't his wife stand behind him during this time?"

"Two good questions. Yes they could and they did. It's amazing what you can do with the courts if you have money and good attorneys. Concerning his wife, no she did not stand behind or beside him or anything else. Before I say something I shouldn't, I will just keep to the known facts. A few days before they finally finished with the courts, my receptionist Anna, ended up having a real problem with her husband and anyway she ran out on him one evening and came to this office to figure things out. She needed to talk to someone and when she couldn't get a hold of me she called Bob's office, and as usual, he was there. Bob treated everyone great but he really liked Anna and she liked him. They often talked in here, and were just good friends, kind of like a father and daughter thing. Anyway, she ended up going over to Bob's office. He talked to her and also talked to her husband on the phone; and they were able to get everything straightened out. As Anna was leaving Bob's office, she gave Bob a big hug thanking him for his help. As she was hugging him,

Anita and Luke pulled up in front of the office and saw them hugging. Anita got out of the car and called them both every name in the book. She told Bob not to bother coming home and promised he would hear from her attorney. Over the next few days, several people tried talking to Anita to explain it was not what she thought. She would have none of it, in fact she accused him of having an affair with me and his own secretary, and two women in the church. It was ugly and it was wrong. A few days later Bob made an appointment with me and brought in divorce papers that Anita had him served with. They were totally unfair and I told him so. He looked at me and said after what Luke had said to him he didn't care anymore."

With a puzzled look on her face Lily asked, "Who is Luke?"

"I can't believe I never told you his son's name. Luke is his son, I am sorry."

"Oh that's all right; I just kept forgetting to ask you. Did Bob tell you what Luke said to him?"

"No, he never did tell me, but I could tell his heart was broken. He had sold all of his equipment for a dime on the dollar and was able to put together enough cash to take care of Anita and Luke for at least a year or two, and paid off their home which he gave to her free and clear. He had a few other legal things he asked me to do for him, and he put an envelope on my desk and asked me to come out front to Anna's desk. He told us both how much he appreciated us, gave us each a hug and we never saw him again."

Annie obviously upset said, "Please excuse me for a minute and left the room."

Lily and Jacob sat there in silence until she came

back. "You really thought a highly of Bob didn't you Annie?"

"Yes I did, he meant a great deal to me, and I still miss him and I wish I would have met him...I'm sorry, I don't need to say anymore. You two have been great for listening to me for so long. Anna is the only other person, besides you two, who knows what I think of him. It's all over now though, we should talk about your meeting with Luke."

"Yes I guess we should, but could I ask you what was in the envelope. None of my business, just curious?"

"Oh, I don't mind telling you. It had a note thanking me for being such a good friend and how he wished things had turned out differently. He also had placed a cashier's check for $2,000 for past and future services. He probably figured if he had just written a regular check I wouldn't cash it. We owed less than $200 on his account, so I put the rest aside in case he ever needed it. As you know we talked a couple times a year, but he never asked for anything like that. In fact, he had me set up an account that he could send money to for Luke's education or anything Luke wanted to use it for. I told Luke about it when he turned 18. He didn't say much when I told him, but said he had received a couple scholarships and grants and was in pretty good shape for college. Every year I sent Luke a copy of the bank statement and he never said anything to me or used any of the money. Bob must have been putting most of his disability check into that account every month, because it is substantial. Typical Bob."

"I know what you mean. I bet in the 15 years I have known him, I didn't see him buy something personal for himself more than five times. He was always buying stuff for other people though. Half the time they didn't even know where it came from."

"OK, I need to tell you a little more about Anita. This almost smacks of gossip but I'm sure it's all public knowledge. As soon as the courts finalized the divorce, Anita and Morgan got married. Don't say anything, I know what you're thinking, I thought the same way. Morgan ended up putting a used car lot together, with money I'm sure he got from Anita. He did fairly well and had built up a profitable business. After about five years, Anita caught him cheating on her. It's kind of ironic that she divorced a good man, who was totally faithful to her, for Morgan. But she did all right in the divorce and it set her up pretty good. A few years later she met a decent guy from the coast and I hear they are doing well. Anyway, I thought I should tell you that before you talk to Luke. When I called Luke and told him about his dad's death, he was obviously remorseful. I told him how sorry I was, especially about them being separated for so long. He said he was sad about that too, and asked if he should do anything. I told him there was nothing I could think of at the time. I told him that you two might be coming to River Bend. He asked me why you would come here, so I told you wanted to piece some of the puzzle together on his dad's life. He said that was probably a good idea. That is a good sign and I think he will be receptive to you this afternoon."

"I am happy to hear that, I had this feeling that it might be a little rough."

"No, I think it will go well. Now you have two options. Luke said you're welcome to go over to his house, or I am offering for all of us to meet her in my office. He said, either way was fine with him. His wife and two kids are out of town so they will not be available for the meeting."

"To tell you the truth, Annie, I would feel a lot better

meeting him here with you. You have done so much already, I hate imposing on you anymore."

"That's quite all right, I don't mind at all."

Lily took out a brochure and said, "One of the people we met on this trip wanted to know if there was any kind of memorial for Bob, and I told her we didn't have anything established. They suggested we put anything people donated into the college fund Bob put together. Pat and I put this little brochure together to let people know about it. I feel kind of awkward though, because it will benefit Jacob. But I was thinking, if by chance enough funds came in, we could open it up to more than just Jacob and Sammy. What do you think?"

"That's a wonderful idea. I like it. What better way to remember someone who had such a heart for kids. In fact, I would love to give the funds that are in that account I set up for Bob with that $2,000 check he gave me before he left umpteen years ago. Believe it or not I think the balance on that account has grown close to $10,000."

"Oh my, that's amazing, and also very generous of you. Are you sure you want to do that? In our neck of the woods that's a lot of money."

"It's a lot of money here, too, but it is not really mine anyway, its Bob's. Let me ask you two questions. First, what do you think Bob would want us to do with it? Secondly, and I hope you're not offended, but how much of the money have you spent ?"

"Not at all. We haven't used any of it. I had some money saved up for a trip. I think you're right, Bob would be pleased about additional funds for education."

"That's what I figured you would say, you're just as much a straight shooter as he was. I will call Luke at work and he will probably come over right after he closes his office at five. His office is just down the street."

"What kind of work does he do?"

"He's a civil engineer. He partnered up with a man who had been here forever. When his partner retired, Luke bought him out. He is doing very well. I understand he has work all over Oregon and Southern Washington."

"I am so glad he is doing well."

"Me too, I think he is a lot like his dad. Let's see, it's 3:30 right now, would you two like to stretch your legs and maybe walk around our little town, then meet back here at five?"

"That would be great; Jacob and I have grown fond of exploring small towns on this trip."

The walk through the town was very good for both Jacob and Lily. It gave them the opportunity to not only see the place Bob called home, but also time to digest all of the information they had learned from Annie. They took their time and did a lot of window shopping and before they knew it was time to head back to Annie's office.

When they arrived in the office Anna said, "Your timing is perfect, Mr. Dolan just got here; please go on back."

As they entered the office Annie was giving Luke a cup of coffee. "Lily and Jacob Fields I would like you meet Luke Dolan."

Lily all of sudden was very weak in the knees and almost shaking. She was amazed how much Luke looked like his father. She could very easily see what Bob looked like 25 years ago. He was very good looking and most important he had his dad's kind eyes. They shook hands and Annie directed everyone to her conference table which had been cleared.

Everyone seemed on edge, so Annie broke the ice. "I don't know about all of you but I've been nervous about this meeting. I know that the circumstances are somewhat awkward but I also know all three of you are very nice people. I would like to start off letting Luke know that the three of us met and talked earlier this afternoon and we are kind of ahead of him in this process. In my mind, this process is putting the pieces of the puzzle together of Bob's life for the last 16 years. He was such a private man that putting that puzzle together has involved Lily and Jacob traveling almost 2,000 miles to meet people who have known your dad over the years. Luke and I don't know much about what has happened the last fifteen years between Denton and Lone Tree and everything in between. So if Luke doesn't mind, and Lily if you and Jacob feel comfortable sharing that with us, it would help us understand things a little better."

Luke's nervousness showed. He looked at Annie, and then Lily and Jacob and said, "If you would please, you are going to fill in a huge void in my life. I would like very much for you to tell us as much as you feel comfortable with, and no detail is too small for me."

"Luke, Jacob and I have had one amazing journey so far to get here. We've met some wonderful people and if you both are up to it we'll tell you everything that comes to our mind starting 15 years ago."

It took almost two hours for Lily and Jacob to tell their story. They all cried and laughed, and finally Lily said, "That's it, that's pretty much it."

Luke listened attentively to all that Lily and Jacob

said. With some hesitation, he said, "I had no idea. I haven't been so teary eyed since my rabbit died when I was a kid."

Everyone laughed and he continued, "It's obvious I had a lot of misconceptions concerning my dad. It's going to take some time for me to sort everything out. With that said, I need to fill in another piece of the puzzle. The last time I saw my Dad I said some things to him that were extremely cruel. In my 12 year old mind, he didn't really care for me and mom, and besides that he was having multiple affairs. Up until I was about ten years old, Dad always wanted to go camping and fishing and sports stuff. Mom didn't care for any of those things, and if she didn't want to go, I didn't either. I guess you could say I was a real momma's boy. The last couple years before he left he became a workaholic. He was always doing something with his business or the church or helping someone. It was uncomfortable of all us when he was home. We just kind of existed those last few years. I didn't know it at the time, but looking back, I'm pretty sure Mom did a good job of turning me against my dad. I don't think she did it on purpose. It just happened. When Annie came to me after my 18th birthday and told me about the trust fund that Dad had set up for me, I was full of emotions. I had put him out of my life and now he was back on my mind. Mom had married and divorced a guy that was kind of a jerk and after Annie told me about the trust fund, I asked Mom if all those things she said about Dad did were true. She broke down crying, and said that they probably weren't but she just had to get out of the rut they were in. She said everything kind of got carried away and the next thing we knew, Dad was gone. Back to the day he left. He came to me to say he was going to be leaving for awhile and that he loved me and would do anything for me. I don't remember exactly what I said, but I do know one thing, now, that I didn't think of then. I have a daughter and a son and if at 12 years old, either one of them said to me what I said to my Dad that day, it would have broken my heart. If my wife divorced me at the same time, I might have done exactly what Dad did. After Annie called to tell me that Dad had died I called Mom and told her. She could tell I was upset and told me that she would probably never forgive herself for what she did to him, and now the only thing she wanted in life was for me to forgive her. She said she robbed me of a relationship with him, and now, after listening to Jacob I feel pretty bad about it myself. I will never be able to get those years back. But that's OK, it's over and I can move on. I can remember him for who he really was and someday I'll be able to share with his grandkids all about their grandpa. It has taken a lot of courage for all three of you to do what you have done and you can rest assured that I will be grateful to you for the rest of my life."

Lily was impressed with this young man who reminded her so much of Bob in his mannerisms, and the way he talked and selected his words. She looked into his eyes and said, "You're an amazing young man and I know your dad kept up on you through Annie. I also knew him well enough to know he had to be very proud of you. No doubt when he found out about your marriage, and then your babies being born. I'm sure it grieved him greatly not to be with you for those special events. I think he was wrong to keep his distance and for not sharing you with Jacob and I, but that's Bob. He would take the pain and live with it before causing for someone else pain. He never had any problem facing off a bully but I guess he couldn't handle confrontation with someone he loved. I didn't realize that until now. I don't know if you will allow it, but I would like to maintain contact with you and your family, pictures of your babies and everything else."

"I would like that very much." Luke replied.

There was a pause and then Annie said, "Luke, your dad left a small amount of money to be used for an education fund for Jacob and Sammy, the girl in Montana. As his son, I should ask you if that is acceptable to you."

Luke looked at her for a few seconds and then said, "Would you please excuse me for a minute? I would like to call my wife. She's at her mother's in Portland."

After Luke left the room with his cell phone in his hand, Annie said, "I hope I didn't offend him by asking him that question."

"I'm sure you didn't, he probably has a relationship with his wife where they discuss just about everything before they make a decision," Lily said.

"I hope that's what it is; he's had a lot laid on him today."

Luke came back into the room and said, "I'm sorry about that, I just needed to talk to my wife for a second about something. First of all, I think it's great that Dad set up the fund for Jacob and Sammy. Earlier I mentioned the fund that he set up for me. Well, I never used any of it. I was able to get through college without it, and it is still there. God has blessed my wife and I with a successful business, and we're well on our way to having our children's college education covered. What I'm trying to say is, that we both would like to donate the balance of that account to my dad's trust fund, if that would be OK."

Annie with a wonderful look of surprise on her face said, "Luke you do realize that that fund has over $35,000 in it?"

"Yes, I do, and I am glad."

After Lily was able to close her mouth she said, "That's totally amazing, I can't believe it! With what has happened on this trip, we are going to be able offer help to several kids. It blows me away!"

"Luke that is truly a beautiful and generous gesture by you and your wife. Your dad would be very proud," Annie said.

"Thank you, Annie. I feel real good about it."

Jacob who had been quietly listening, stepped up to Luke and said, "Luke I have something that I hope you will accept. Mom and I have discussed it and we would like you to have this." Jacob handed Luke his father's little wooden box.

Luke opened the box and took out his dad's passport, then the Bronze Star, and finally the two Purple Hearts. Luke was caught off guard and just stood there looking at his gift, then, with a voice filled with emotion, said, "You couldn't have given me a more precious gift. I don't know what to say. Until you told me I didn't know anything about Dad's time in Vietnam. I don't think mom even knew about it. Thank you very much."

"We are glad you like it, but it going to cost you. You must send us pictures of your family."

"I will, right away."

———

The next day Jacob drove for four hours before they stopped for lunch. During that four hours Lily wrote in one of her notebooks, non-stop. She did the same for the rest of that day and most of the next. When then pulled into their driveway late the next evening they had finished a most extraordinary journey.

CHAPTER 26

The morning rush was over and Lily and Lucy were enjoying a cup of coffee. It had been six months since Lily and Jacob had taken their life changing road trip. The sun was warm and life was good.

The front door opened and a man came in. He had a warm smile and soft eyes. He sat down at the counter and ordered coffee.

Lily poured him a cup and asked, "What brings you to these parts, mister?"

"Just traveling around, enjoying the country."

"Headed for any place in particular?"

"No, I retired a few months ago and I'm just out looking around."

"I hope you don't think I am nosey, but that's all you do, look around."

The stranger laughed and said, "I guess just driving around, looking, sounds a little odd. I have always wanted to write a book about a character in the modern day west. I've been in Montana, Wyoming, and Colorado and now I'm here. Just haven't found what or who I am looking for yet. Not in a hurry though. If I keep lookin, I will find something to write about."

"Have you written much before?"

"Nope, this will be my first project."

"How do you know if you are any good?"

"I don't, but will never know till I give it try."

"Where are you heading from here?"

"Don't know yet, maybe south."

Lily studied the man's eyes and said, "Will you do me a favor, mister?"

"Be glad to, if I can."

Lily filled his coffee cup and said, "I'll be right back."

Lily came back a few minutes later and put three, well worn notebooks on the counter in front him.

"What do you have here ma'am?"

"If you have time I would like you to look at this material. They are labeled one, two, and three. If you want to look at them, read them in that order and tell me what you think."

"It would be my pleasure, how long will you be here?"

"Till eight."

"It will cost you dinner."

"Deal!"

The man left and nine hours later he came back into the diner. He sat at the counter and Lily poured him a cup of coffee.

"Find anything interesting in there?"

The man took a sip of his coffee and said, "Is this material based on facts or just out of someone's imagination?"

"It's the real deal, I wrote all of it."

"Well I'm not sure what you have in mind, but if you would consider letting me turn it into a book, you would make my day. Shoot, you would make my whole year."

"I have a few questions first," Lily said, "Who is Jesus Christ to you, where do you sleep at night, and I guess I should ask your name?"

"He is my Lord and Savior and the most important thing in my life! I have my van set up to camp out of and my name is Dave."

"Here is a key to a travel trailer out back, you're welcome to it as long as you like and my name is not ma'am, it's Lily. Oh, by the way, we're having church right here in this diner tomorrow morning at ten o'clock, if you would like to come."

THE END